Killing Rosa

A Kell Digby Crime Novel

Lynn Kear

ALSO BY LYNN KEAR

Black-Hearted Bitch

Relative Innocence

Tighter, Tighter

Murder in a Buckhead Garden

Laurette Taylor: American Stage Legend

Evelyn Brent: The Life and Times of Hollywood's Lady Crook

The Complete Kay Francis Career Record: All Film, Stage, Radio and Television Appearances

Kay Francis: A Passionate Life and Career

FIRST EDITION

THIS IS A WORK OF FICTION. NAMES, CHARACTERS, PLACES, AND INCIDENTS ARE THE PRODUCT OF THE AUTHOR'S IMAGINATION OR ARE USED FICTITIOUSLY. ANY RESEMBLANCE TO ACTUAL PERSONS, LIVING OR DEAD, BUSINESS ESTABLISHMENTS, EVENTS, OR LOCALES IS ENTIRELY COINCIDENTAL.

Printed in the United States of America

COVER DESIGNER: KV HERNDON

Copyright © 2014 Lynn Kear
All rights reserved.
ISBN: 0615945856
ISBN-13: 978-0615945859
Grey Fedora Books

For Kimber

ACKNOWLEDGMENTS

Thanks to Risa Rispoli for participating in the Golden Crown Literary Society's Character Auction.

Drue Barrett, once again, saved me from Microsoft Word hell. I owe her Waffle House for life.

Special thanks to Kimber Herndon for editing, proofing, and creating the cover design.

ONE

"Who are you really, honey?"

Debra Palmer leveled the gun at my bare chest. Sprawled in her king-sized bed, I focused on her eyes, not the gun. It wasn't a big scary gun. It was a little puny thing, but, hey, a gun is a gun.

I was Mandy for this job. Larry was Mack. Mack and Mandy. Cute, huh? Larry wanted to use Mack and Mabel because he's a movie buff, and these are the names of a long-forgotten Hollywood couple that no one cares about except Larry.

"No one will buy that my name is Mabel," I said.

Larry looks like a Mack, though. He's a big, muscular guy with a shaved head and gorilla arms.

He really wanted me to be Mabel. "I'll be Mack. You be Mabel," I said.

We argued back and forth until he finally got it through his thick skull that I wasn't on board with Mabel. We compromised on Mandy.

I was pissed off because Debra could have done the drama before we had sex. The sex wasn't terrible, but it wasn't my idea. Mrs. Palmer was old enough to be my mother. If I cheated on Gretchen, it'd be with someone who made me wet. Not that Mrs. Palmer wasn't attractive. She was. Debra was charming, intelligent, and had a rocking body. Most would call her beautiful. To make things even more interesting, she was good in bed. Still, if I'd known she'd pull a gun, I wouldn't have slept with the bitch.

I didn't think she'd shoot me. She had a lot to lose. She was the wife of one of the richest men in the state. Her husband was running for governor, for Christ's sake. She had to know she'd never get away with it. This was a bluff, a game. She was used to expensive, one-of-a-kind things. I was a toy.

Life was a lot less dangerous when I was a fucking hit man. It was that damn Larry Howell who'd gotten me into this mess. He's my brother-in-law, and since we met we've been on a two-person crime spree that would have horrified Gin and Gretchen. Gin is my sister. She thought Larry was a criminal justice consultant and I was a security consultant who occasionally worked for him. Something or other. We were always vague.

Gretchen is my partner and Gin's best friend since kindergarten. Like I said, if either had a clue what we were really up to, Larry and I would be in huge trouble. Gretchen and Gin are respectable people. College professors. It would rock their worlds. They'd dump our asses too. Larry and I would be doomed to lying around in our sweats, watching sports on TV, eating potato chips and drinking beer, blaming each other for messing up a good thing.

It's difficult to explain what Larry does. He calls it "quasi-legal." He specializes in getting guys who've got it coming, people who should have been arrested and imprisoned long ago. Getting them good. It's a lucrative business. Clients come to Larry with motivation, information, and lots of money to screw someone. Not literally. Figuratively. After Larry's done, the target is ruined and often in jail.

The first time I worked with Larry, we demolished a crooked hedge fund dude. That one took months of planning. This one didn't. Still, it seemed foolproof until Mrs. Palmer got it in her head that she wanted to fuck me.

Her husband Wallace Palmer owns a health insurance

company, and, like I said, is running for governor. John Reynolds also wants to be governor, so he's hired Larry to ruin Palmer. Fortunately, Wally's made it easy. He's having affairs with two strippers, a teenage intern, and the COO of his company. Three of these are dudes, and if you correctly guess the three I'll be surprised.

The con is a beaut. Larry's sold himself as a computer expert to Palmer and offered to set up a program to access every file, email—everything— Reynolds has on his computer. It's amazing how eager people are to destroy others. Reynolds isn't much better. He's a sleaze bucket, but who else would get involved in something like this?

Earlier today, Larry went alone to the Palmer's white Greek Revival on Tuxedo Drive and pretended to "check out the specs" on Palmer's computer. He then installed a "custom program" that would supposedly copy and send files from Reynolds' computer to Palmer's.

After the installation, Larry met me at our Buckhead hotel where he downloaded like crazy on his laptop, while I, acting as Larry's assistant, returned to the Palmer residence. My job was to keep Mrs. Palmer from logging on to the computer until Larry remotely copied all the data.

I was at the PC in Palmer's basement office, pretending to do something or other while staring at the screen. It didn't matter because Debra wasn't the least bit interested in anything but me. After I made sure the program was sending data to Larry, I told Debra some mumbo jumbo about how I'd done something on the computer and needed to wait several hours until it finished running.

She invited me up to her kitchen for a cup of coffee and a piece of peach pie. I ate the pie and sipped the coffee while she brought out an old issue of *Veranda*. She flipped through the pages and then laid the magazine in front of me. It was open to a two-page spread on her house in St. Simon's. The beach house was sweet, but it was like watching someone else's home movies. Just when I willed myself not to yawn, she rubbed against me, touched my hand, that sort of thing. Finally, she put her arms around me and nuzzled my neck. Subtle, she wasn't. I had time to kill, so I went to bed with her in the fancy upstairs bedroom. Big mistake, and here I am with a gun pointing at me.

I widened my eyes, hoping she'd think it was an expression of fear. Maybe she'd feel sorry for me.

Nope. She brought up the gun until it was aimed at my face. Really? My *face*? Shoot my fucking face?

She stepped back. I've been told I have a scary look. She lowered the gun until it once again pointed at my chest.

"Put down the gun," I said, sensing I had the upper hand.

We remained at a stalemate for several minutes. I tried to recreate whatever she'd seen on my face, but apparently it's a natural expression, something I can't control.

"This doesn't seem to be your thing, Mandy," she said.

"It's not."

She set the gun on her dresser and came back to bed. It wasn't my thing, but it was hers. She turned into a dynamo, and we went at it good. She didn't mention the gun again, nor did I. As you can probably guess, I was eager to leave.

"Hey, Mandy," she said, just before I walked out, "how about giving me your phone number? Maybe we can get together again."

"I'm seeing someone," I said. "I can't give you my number. I'll take yours and call when I can."

I typed her number into my phone and saved it under Debra. It made her happy. I went out to my rental and headed back to Larry and the hotel.

"You took a long time," he said, when I walked in the room. "I was getting worried."

"I got tied up," I said.

"Everything's in place," he said. "We need to get out of

here."

"Fine by me."

Larry had told Palmer it'd take a week before he finalized the job. That would give Larry enough time to find what he was looking for and then give it to whomever could nail Palmer. Larry never went into detail about this part. I assumed he had someone at the FBI or in law enforcement who took stuff and then used it to get a search warrant or subpoena or something. There was a lot that Larry didn't tell me, which was fine with me. I didn't give a fuck.

Anyway, by the time Palmer gets suspicious, the program will be gone from his computer without a trace. When Palmer tries to explain the con to the authorities, he'll sound like a madman. Actually, he might not try too hard to explain because he'll have to admit that he tried to hack into Reynolds' computer. Like I said, this one is a beaut.

I took a quick shower, and we packed up. I followed Larry in my Mustang to return his rental. He turned in the car, and we headed to the Atlanta airport.

"I had sex with her," I said.

Larry was driving my Mustang because men like to drive. It was fine with me because I was busy deleting Debra's phone number from my contacts.

Larry shot me a look of disapproval. "Why?" he asked.

"I hadn't killed enough time. She asked."

"You're not supposed to do that."

"You told me to keep her out of the way."

"What will you tell Gretchen?"

I snorted. "I'm not telling her."

He shook his head. "Women find out this stuff," he said, quickly pulling the car off the road.

We were at a strip mall called Lucky East that had a nail salon, a dentist's office, and three other storefronts that were advertised as available.

"Tell me everything," he said. "How much trouble are we in?"

"It's cool," I said, wondering if there was a Lucky West.

"Kell."

I didn't appreciate his tone, so I turned my body and looked out the window. Larry can be a girly man sometimes. He's a worrier, and, frankly, it irritated me.

"Kell," he said. "What do you mean, she pulled a gun on you?"

"During sex. She got out of bed and pulled a gun on me. She asked me who I really was."

"A loaded gun?"

"I assume it was loaded."

"A Glock?"

"A pea shooter. A .22."

"What did you tell her?"

"Nothing. She realized I wasn't turned on. She put down the gun and came back to bed."

He thought about it for a minute. "She must be crazy."

"To sleep with me?"

"No. To pull a gun on you. That's crazy." He paused. "She's old enough to be your mother. Holy smokes. Pulled a gun on you? That woman's nuts."

"I'm more afraid of Gretchen."

"You really had sex with Mrs. Palmer?"

"Yes."

"I mean—"

"On the bed. Naked. Sex." I turned to him. "What girls do in those porno films you watch."

"Wow." He chuckled. "You really think you can keep it from Gretchen?"

"I have to."

I used to be a dirty dog, and I still have it in me. Gretchen is the first serious relationship I've had unless you count Rosa, and you can't because we were never really together. When Gretchen moved in with me, she told me the worst thing I could do was cheat. The second worst thing was lie. I think it was in that order. I've been lying big-time for a while. I haven't cheated until now.

"How was she?" he asked. "Mrs. Palmer?"

I smiled and winked.

"Wow," he said. Like most guys, Larry has a thing about lesbians. He tries to hide it, but he's intrigued. It drives Gin nuts. "How'd she approach you?"

"She asked me to go to bed with her. When I hesitated, she implied I was insulting her."

"You think she's a lesbian?"

"I think she's bi."

He thought for a moment. "She pulled the gun on you during sex?"

"Yes. Then she had sex with me again."

"So you think she planned—"

"I think she planned on fucking me and then playing a game. Like I said, it seemed to be her thing."

"It's a thing?"

I shrugged. "People like what they like."

"How old do you think she is?"

"Fifties."

"I was thinking older."

"Really?"

"Yeah," Larry said. "Palmer's about sixty-five. Is that the oldest you've—"

"No." Like I said, I used to be dirty dog.

"You need to write a book one day, Kell."

He started up the car again, and we got back on the road. He got out at the airport, gave me $50,000 cash, and we said goodbye. I headed back to Stone Mountain where I live with Gretchen. He caught a flight back to California.

TWO

Gretchen thought I'd been in Dallas for two days with Larry to consult with a client on a security system. Heading back on 285, supposedly from the airport, I called and asked if she wanted me to pick up dinner at Harmony, our favorite vegetarian restaurant. She was thrilled. I picked up mock Mongolian beef and sweet and sour ribs. I also swung by the Costco in Brookhaven and picked up a chocolate cheesecake.

Larry and I had gotten away with our stuff for a while, partly because we were careful what we told Gin and Gretchen. This time I was careless. I'm a stickler for details, so I'm not sure how it happened, but I fucked up.

Gretchen and I chowed down on dinner and then ate the cheesecake in the family room in front of the TV. We were watching an episode of *International House Hunters*. A couple was looking to buy a beach house in Costa Rica. "Nice, very nice," we kept saying. I figured we'd finish our cheesecake and then go upstairs and get reacquainted.

"So Larry was with you?" she asked during a Lowe's commercial.

"Yeah. Driving me crazy too, talking about Oceanvue." This was the university where he and Gin worked. Gretchen was teaching there when I met her. She and Gin were full-time professors, and Larry was adjunct which meant he taught one or two classes each semester. "I only listened to half of it, but the gist of it was that he doesn't like his department chair, and they want him to teach all his classes online."

Gretchen was interested in what I was saying, so I kept talking. "It wouldn't be so bad, but you know how he feels about classroom interaction. You just don't get that online."

"Did he say anything about what Gin's doing?"

I thought it an odd question. Hell, she talked to Gin a few times a week, but doofus me kept going. "Yeah. He said she's also being forced to do more online courses. She feels the same way, but what you gonna do?"

"He talked about this in Dallas?"

In that instant, I knew I was cooked.

"Kell?"

"Yeah."

"Are you having an affair?" she asked.

I'm good about having a stone face when I need one, but I almost fell off the couch. I gasped, and I'm not a gasper.

My first reaction was to lie. "No. Why ask me something like that?"

She muted the TV and narrowed her eyes at me. The look on her face was, 'You not only slept with someone. You lied about it when I asked.'

Gretchen is easy to read. If a movie is on, you can watch her moon face and know what is happening.

"Try telling the truth, Kell."

I went with my robot voice. "I-have-no-idea-why-you-think-I—"

"You told me you were with Larry. You weren't. The only reason you'd lie is because you were with someone."

Fucking fuckster. Larry and I hadn't gotten our fucking stories straight. Now I was fucked. If I said Larry was lying, then he'd be in trouble with Gin. It was me or Larry.

I had to take the hit. Gretchen had me. I'd cheated, and I'd lied. The two worst things I could have done to her.

"I made a mistake," I said. "It was one time, and it—" I almost said it meant nothing, but Gin told me that women hated hearing that. Not that they want to hear it was the best fucking experience you've ever had, but this wouldn't fly. "It was a mistake. I'm sorry."

I didn't do a great job of easing the tension.

"Is it the first time?" she asked in the metallic voice she uses when she's on the verge of yelling.

"Yes. Absolutely. And the last." I wasn't one hundred percent sure about this, of course, but it seemed important to say it. "I wish it'd never happened."

"I do too. Are you in touch with her?"

"No. It was a one-time thing. It's over. I won't have any contact with her."

"Can I look at your phone?"

Was I always this stupid? I mean, holy fucking God, was I taking stupid pills? I walked into every trap she set. The only incriminating thing on my phone were texts to and from Larry. But some of them would make Gretchen wonder. She'd say something to Gin, Gin would ask Larry, and we'd both be in for it.

I still hadn't said anything. She held out her hand.

"I haven't been in contact with her," I said. "You'll have to trust me."

She gave me a 'Give me a break' look. "You won't let me see your phone."

"I'm not seeing her. I'm not in contact with her."

"Since when? I mean, you just came back from seeing her. Right? Does she live in Dallas? Or is that a lie too? Do you have a receipt for your plane ticket?"

I sat mute.

"Why'd you do it?" she asked.

Honestly, what could I say? "She wanted to," I said, knowing it was dumb before I said it.

Gretchen's eyes opened wide, and she made a frustrated sound. "That's lame."

"It was in the moment," I said, wanting to immediately tape my mouth shut. Frankly, I wanted it behind us, never to talk about it again.

"Kell, tell me how many times you've cheated since we've been together."

"I swear to you it's the only time. I swear to God."

"I don't understand how you could do it. Did you think about me?"

"Yes. Of course. I regretted it immediately."

"Okay. All right."

I didn't like the way she said it. Like she'd decided something. Gretchen sat back and crossed her arms. None of this was good.

"I'm sorry," I said. "I won't do it again."

"It's fine."

Rosa once told me that these were the two worst words a woman could say to you. Especially if she repeated them.

"It's fine," Gretchen said again. "Really. It's fine."

It would have been better if she screamed at me.

"I'm calling Gin," she said.

"Please don't tell her." I actually put my hands together like I was praying. "Please, Gretchen. Don't tell her."

"I need someone to talk to."

I'm not proud to say I got on my knees. "Not her. Talk to me. Tell me how I can make things right."

Gretchen shook her head. "I need to call her."

"Please. Anyone but her. Talk to someone else."

"It's humiliating. Do you have any idea how this makes me feel? I'm not enough for you. It's degrading." She was wound up again but closed her eyes and willed herself to calm down. "It's fine," Gretchen said and patted my head.

She left the room and walked into the kitchen. I couldn't hear her exact words, but she'd gotten Gin on the phone. Meanwhile, I snuck upstairs and called Larry.

"I'm fucked, Larry," I said. "Gretchen thinks I'm having an affair." I was talking fast. "You said we were supposed to say we were together on this one."

"No. Remember. I said I told Gin I was in Nevada for a convention. We talked about this, Kell. I've got pamphlets and stuff to show her. Didn't you come up with something?"

I thought for a moment. He was right. As much as I hated to admit it, he was right.

"I fucked up," I said.

He already knew, picking it up from Gin's side of the conversation. "I don't know how it happened, Kell. I owe you one." He said this because he didn't want me to sacrifice him.

"Yeah."

"Thank you so much for not putting it on me."

"Uh-huh. She's angry, Larry."

"Gin will leave me, Kell." He was panicky. "There's no question in my mind. Be good to Gretchen and give her some time and space."

Larry was a good guy, but too afraid of Gin to say anything.

"Do a Kobe and buy her jewelry or something," he said.

"That won't work, Larry."

"Come on. You know her. Say or do whatever you need to."

"She's gone all silent on me. What are you hearing on your side?"

He didn't want to tell me.

"Is it bad?" I asked.

"Give her time. She's ranting and raving now."

"You can hear her?"

"Gin."

"Fuck."

"She'll calm down. Isn't there anything you could give

Gretchen that would make her happy, make her forget? A trip to Hawaii?"

"She doesn't care about things like that."

Larry said more meaningless things. He was trying to be supportive but was mostly glad it wasn't him. We hung up.

I turned to go back downstairs. Gretchen stood in the doorway.

"Who were you talking to?" she asked.

"When?"

"Just now. You heard me coming upstairs and hung up real quick."

I acted like I didn't understand.

"I heard you talking on the phone, Kell." She was on the verge of going rabid on me. "Did you call her?"

"No."

"Who were you talking to?"

For the love of God. I looked at the ceiling and rolled my eyes. Gretchen misunderstood. She thought I was mocking her. I was actually mocking myself for being such a dumbass.

"Am I bothering you?" she asked. "Do you want me to just shut up and let you talk to your girlfriend?"

"I wasn't talking to my girlfriend."

She held out her hand. "Let me see your phone." If she saw that I'd called Larry, she'd probably be relieved, but also wonder why. Knowing Gretchen, she'd assume I called to ask him to lie for me. That'd open up a huge can of worms. She'd wonder how many times Larry had lied for me. Then Gin would get involved. She'd have a fucking fit if she thought Larry had covered for me.

"Where does she live?" Gretchen asked.

I didn't answer, and she lost it. "You are so fucking disrespectful to me." Gretchen doesn't swear a lot. Especially compared to me.

"It was a one-night stand," I said. "There's no relationship."

"It was a *two*-night stand. And you were just talking to her on the phone. What did you tell her? That your bitch of a girlfriend was giving you a hard time?"

"I would never talk about you like that. You've got this all wrong, Gretchen."

"Where does she live? Atlanta?" She laughed, but it wasn't a happy laugh. "God, I'm such a fool. Where does she live?"

"I swear to you it's not an affair. It was a mistake. A one-night stand. A stupid thing. I love you. You're the person I want to be with."

"You think you're slick, don't you?"

"Obviously not."

"You think this is funny?"

"No."

I've seen Gretchen angry, but not like this. I suspected Gin amped her up.

"Confess everything to me," she said. "Then I'll decide what to do."

"What do you mean?"

She started to cry. I hugged her, but she wriggled free and gave me a hateful, cold look.

"I met someone in the park," I said, starting to talk, making it up as I went along. "One day when I was walking."

"When you were with Thuggie?" She was appalled that the dog was part of the story.

I nodded. "She lives in Atlanta. I went to see her, but it's over."

"You were in Atlanta?"

"Yes."

"What's her name?"

"Debra."

"How long have you known her?"

"A very short time. It's not a big romantic affair, Gretchen. I swear to you. A stupid one-night stand."

"Quit saying that. It's *two* nights. At least. You talked to her tonight?"

I hesitated before I lied some more. "I told her you found out. I'd already told her I couldn't see her again. I told her you might contact her. You wanted my phone. You might start calling."

This was plausible to Gretchen. She thought for a moment. "How old is she?" she asked.

"Older than you."

"How much older?"

"I don't want to talk about her. Honestly. I want to be with you."

"How much older?"

"Lots older."

This surprised her. "What's lots?" she asked, narrowing her eyes.

"I didn't ask—"

"How old is she?"

I shrugged. "I don't know. Forties, I guess."

"How many times have you done this?"

"One time. I'm not like that."

"I'm trying to remember how many times you've traveled." Gretchen started counting on her fingers. She stopped for a moment and lowered a finger. "That time I know you were with Larry."

I took her hand. She pulled her hand back.

"I'm telling you the truth," I said. "This is the first time."

"Were you planning to tell me?"

She started crying again. Sobbing, she covered her face with her hands. I felt like a schmuck.

"I didn't want to hurt you," I said. "I knew I'd screwed up."

She kept crying. I got panicky. This could be a long night if it didn't get better.

"Tell me what I can do to make it right," I said. "I'll do anything."

I lightly touched her arm. She took her hands off her face, glared at me, and clomped downstairs.

A few moments later, I went downstairs and found her in the family room picking up our plates. She headed into the kitchen. I followed.

"It's fine," she said, standing at the sink. "It's the way you are."

"It's not fine. I'm sorry."

"I know you are." At least she wasn't yelling anymore. "It's the way you are. Gin said it too. 'What did you expect?' That's what Gin said."

Thanks a lot, Gin. "I'll make it up to you," I said.

She nodded and put the dishes in the dishwasher and then walked to the powder room off the kitchen. Using toilet paper, she blew her nose and threw the tissue in the garbage.

"I'm going to bed," she said.

I followed her upstairs. "Are you okay?" I asked in our room.

"Yeah. I'm okay. It's all okay. It's fine."

"What will happen?"

She shrugged. "I guess we'll go on like we have. That's what you want, isn't it?"

It sounded like a trick question. She started undressing.

"Will you let Thuggie out before you go to bed?" she asked.

"Sure."

Gretchen climbed into bed. Thuggie jumped in next to her.

"Come on, boy," I said. "Want to go out?"

He jumped off the bed and followed me downstairs and then outside. By the time we came back upstairs, the light was out in the bedroom, and Gretchen lay on her side.

"Gretchen," I said, when I got in bed. I lightly touched her shoulder with my fingertips. Believe it or not, I still thought I could get some.

"I don't want to talk about it anymore," she said. "I just want to go to sleep."

I moved my fingertips down to the small of her back. She drew away. Thuggie saw his opportunity and wedged himself between us. He's like that.

THREE

Gretchen changed her mind about wanting to talk. She didn't even let me fully wake up the next morning before she started firing questions.

"When did you meet her?" she asked.

I had to make up something. "A month ago."

"You've been talking since then?"

"Gretchen, I don't think the details are important."

That was the wrong thing to say.

"Maybe they're not important to you, but they are to me," she snapped.

"We haven't been talking."

"When did you decide you had to be with her?" she asked.

The whole thing was getting more and more out of control. In the past, I would have left. I don't like arguing. If a woman started this stuff with me before Gretchen, I was out the door. One problem this time is it's my house. It'd also make Gretchen even angrier.

"Kell?"

I put my hands out like I had no idea, couldn't even begin to guess.

"I never noticed you acting any different," Gretchen said. She gave a short laugh. "Were you emailing her too?"

"No."

"Can I check your computer?" she asked.

"Knock yourself out."

She was surprised I gave her the okay. I'll be damned if she didn't go to the PC and log in to my email. I frantically tried to remember if there was anything the least bit incriminating. Larry and I don't communicate via email for obvious reasons. While Gretchen went to my Sent file, I made a mental note to start deleting this stuff. Anyway, most of the emails were to Gin. There were others, but none were sent to anyone Gretchen didn't know.

"Do you want to read them?" I asked.

I shouldn't have been snarky. She was relieved but sad.

"Gretchen, I'm telling you, it was no big thing. No big romance. Not at all."

"Then why'd you go see her? Why do it? Why risk losing everything for something that was no big deal?"

"I was stupid."

"I'm leaving for work." She dressed and left.

I immediately phoned Larry again. He told me Gretchen called Gin after she left the house.

"They're ratcheting each other up," he warned.

I didn't know what to expect when Gretchen returned home that evening, but she was remarkably cool. Looking back, I should have known something was up.

Over the next couple weeks, I convinced myself I'd squared things with her. She was icy, but that was to be expected. She wasn't yelling or crying or anything like that. She was pleasant. Not overly so, but polite. She turned down sex a few times, but I thought it was a matter of her needing time before things were right. She wasn't mean about it, but was clear there'd be none of that. She continued to kiss me goodbye in the morning, and, like I said, was civil. I figured I'd get the frigid act for maybe another week, then things would be okay again.

Meanwhile, the story broke about Wallace Palmer. Larry had used an anonymous email account to send filthy emails between Wally and his fuck buddies to the *Atlanta Journal-Constitution*, hoping they'd bite and publish an article. They were too chicken. However, when Palmer was indicted for embezzling from his company, they couldn't wait to pile on.

I watched Gretchen read the articles and wondered if she'd make the connection between Debra and Atlanta. She didn't. Of course, it'd be a stretch for her to guess that this was my Debra. We didn't talk about the story, but she shook her head and muttered, "What a jerk," when she read about Palmer's transgressions.

Palmer withdrew from the campaign and announced his resignation from the health care company "to spend more time with his family." Debra, however, didn't do the nicey-wifey thing. She kicked him out of the house and started divorce proceedings. Indictments kept coming. He claimed it was all politically motivated, which it was, but it wouldn't have been successful if he hadn't been a dirty dog. Anyway, if you're interested, John Reynolds is now leading the Georgia gubernatorial polls.

Gin quizzed Larry several times about how much he knew about my affairs. Yes. Now it was affairs. According to Larry, Gin was convinced I'd been cheating on Gretchen for some time. She was also convinced that Larry knew more than he was telling. He claimed ignorance.

"I hope it works out," he said. I had the feeling he knew something that he wasn't telling me. He did.

FOUR

"I'm leaving you, Kell. You'll never change."

Gretchen must have made up her mind the day she found out about the cheating thing. She'd finished the semester at the community college and had the summer off. If she'd broken up with me during the semester, there'd be too much drama. So she waited. And planned. Then she let me have it.

"It'll happen again," she said, arms folded, head tilted. "I should have realized you weren't the type to settle down, but I wanted to believe you." I had the feeling these words had been reinforced by Gin. They had my sister's accent.

Gretchen calmly told me she was driving to California with the dog and cat and would be in contact with me later about her final decision.

"I'll think about things and decide whether I should resign from my position and move back to California. I'm too upset right now to make a good decision. If I decide to stay in Georgia, I'm moving out."

She had a script and got through it without going all emotional. I sat with my mouth open, taking it all in.

I was in a routine. The moment I learned I was being dumped, I was getting ready to take Thuggie to Stone Mountain

Park for a walk. We did this every morning around eleven. In fact, while Gretchen was talking to me, he watched me like a hawk, expecting me to get his leash any second.

"I'm not getting into a big money thing with you," she said. "We can resolve this in a mature, responsible way."

I still hadn't said anything.

"I know most of the money is yours," she said. "I'll try to backtrack and figure out what I brought in—"

I waved my hand. "I don't care about that. I told you I was sorry."

"I'll make payments on the car," she said. "We can work things out in a fair, equitable manner."

"I gave you that car as a gift. You don't have to pay me back."

She felt sorry for me. "At some point we can talk, but I want some time. I'm staying with Gin in Oceanvue. Don't call unless it's an emergency. When I'm ready, I'll call. I'm serious, Kell. No fucking games."

"You're leaving today?"

"Right now. The car's packed." That would have been no small job. The car was a green and white Mini Cooper. I'd gifted it to her on her last birthday because she'd remarked lots of times about how cute they were. If you knew Gretchen, you'd know it was the perfect car for her.

She'd moved from California in a Subaru SUV with a U-Haul. After I bought her the Mini Cooper, she insisted on selling the Subaru because she felt guilty having two cars. She gave the money to me. I didn't need it. I'm loaded. But it was important to her. It didn't make any difference because we have a joint checking account, which was where I deposited the money.

Right now, though, I'll bet she wished she still had the Subaru. It wouldn't be a Sunday school picnic taking Thuggie and Bella on a road trip all the way across the United States. In fact, it made me briefly wonder if I'd subconsciously gotten her the Mini

Cooper so she couldn't leave. Let's be honest. There's no way the Coop will haul her stuff back to California. It'll blow out its little mini engine if it tries to pull a U-Haul all the way to Oceanvue.

"There's nothing I can say—"

"Nothing." Her voice broke, and she quickly snatched Thuggie's leash from the doorknob in the kitchen. Thuggie doesn't care who he goes with. He jumped up and down, thrilled to death. I gave him a dirty look, but he acted like he didn't see it. I watched from the front door while Gretchen led Thuggie to her car and then let him jump in the backseat. He gleefully stood up so he could look out the window at my sad, pathetic ass.

Gretchen returned, got the cat carrier, and hissed something in a low voice to Bella. It was probably something about not fucking with her. Bella has a bad attitude. Gretchen grabbed her up without too much damage, squeezed her fat ass in the carrier, and then walked past me, struggling with the crate. I didn't offer to help.

Gretchen tottered out to her car and then came back and shut the front door without saying a word. The car started and drove off. I sat on the couch and didn't move for a long time.

Finally, when I didn't know what else to do, I called Gin. "What the fuck?" I asked.

"It's been building up," Gin said. "The cheating, the lies. Yeah, she'd finally had it. She couldn't get past it. She decided the night you told her. She just wanted to keep the peace until the semester was over."

"Why didn't you give me a heads up?"

"It's not my place."

She's known Gretchen longer than me because she and I only recently found out about each other. It's obvious who she's loyal to. In many ways, Gretchen is more like her sister than me.

"I don't want to break up with her, Gin," I said. "Give me some advice." She didn't say anything for a long time. "Gin?"

"I don't know what to tell you, Kell. Trust is important to

her."

"I made a mistake. I'm not perfect, but I'm remorseful."

"She figures you'll do it again. And apologize again. Not a pattern she wants to get into."

"If Larry cheated, would you give him a second chance?"

"Absolutely not," she said, angry just thinking about it. "No way."

"You don't think she'll start missing me and change her mind?"

"I can't predict the future."

"Yeah, but what do you think?"

"I think she's over it. We've talked a lot over the past couple weeks. Once Gretchen makes a decision, that's it."

I started crying. It made Gin uncomfortable, but I couldn't help it. I bawled like a little kid until I finally pulled myself together. "All right. I appreciate your honesty. Thanks for listening."

"Call if you need to," she said.

"Uh-huh." I lost my temper. "I can't believe how cold you're being."

That set her off. She'd been on the verge and couldn't control herself anymore.

"What in the fuck were you thinking, Kell?" she asked.

"B—"

"You *cheated* on her. You lied to her. You treated her horribly."

"I—"

"You think I'm cold. She's devastated. I feel responsible. I told her to go for it. I didn't think you were relationship material, but I—"

"Y—"

"Don't fucking interrupt me. I knew in my heart you couldn't do it. There's something wrong with you. I'm sorry if I'm hurting your feelings, but you've got a chip missing. This will change our relationship too. She's my best friend. You've fucked up her life. She left her job and family to be with you. You pull something like this. Honest to God, Kell, what were you thinking?"

She wouldn't let me say anything, so I stayed quiet.

"You had a good thing with her," she said. "I hope you learn from this, but I doubt you will."

Gin hung up on me.

I spent the next few days hoping hard that Gretchen would call. Hopefully, once she got to California, Gin would tell her I was a basket case. She didn't call.

My everyday routine was shot to hell. I didn't want to eat. I didn't want to read. I didn't turn on the TV. I didn't talk to anyone. Gretchen and I had friends we hung out with, but I certainly didn't want to tell them what had happened.

I took long walks in the park, though it wasn't the same without my former loyal buddy, Thuggie. I've been through break-ups before, but those relationships were short-term affairs, things that weren't a good idea to begin with. This one put me through some changes. It was my fault. Gin was right. I had something good, and I blew it.

I kept having the same thoughts in my head. Over and over. I couldn't stop. Someone needed to shoot me in my fucking head. Since there were no volunteers, I did the next best thing. I called Rosa in Miami.

FIVE

"Hey, sweetie, what's up?" Rosa asked.

"Gretchen left me."

"The woman who moved in with you?"

She knew damn well who Gretchen was.

It was quiet for a long time.

"Why?" she finally asked.

"She thinks I had an affair."

"Why would she think that?"

"I had sex with someone."

"You told her?"

"She found out. I'm torn up about it, Rosa."

"I'm sorry. Poor baby got her heart broken. She'll come back."

"I don't know."

"For you, she will. Of course, she will." Her voice soothed.

"She went to California. I'm not allowed to call. I'm going crazy. My sister's on her side." I sounded like a punk.

"Let me call you back, sweetie. I'm driving. I'll call you when I get home."

We hung up. I didn't have anything else to do, so I sat and waited.

"I'm home now," Rosa said, two hours later when she called

back. "Do you want to get back together with her?"

"Hell, yes." I laid down on the couch and hung my feet over one end.

"Give her space. Give it time. Look, I know you're probably having a meltdown. Why don't you come down here? It'll do you good. I'll make sure you eat right and get some sleep. Are you back on Cocoa Puffs?"

"No." The last time I had a meltdown, Rosa was able to fix me. She'd arrived at my house and found me skinny and unkempt, surviving on white toast and Cocoa Puffs.

"Are you eating?" she asked.

"Yes."

"Kell?"

"Not a lot, but I'm eating."

"Come down here and let me make sure you're okay," she said. "I can't come there. Too much work. I'm worried about you. Come to Miami, and I'll make sure you get what you need."

I hesitated less than a second. Fuck it. "Okay."

"I'll book a flight," she said. "I know how much you hate doing that kind of thing. I'll pay for it too. I want to see you, make sure you're okay. You sound a little crazy."

Rosa used to handle my travel arrangements because I can't be bothered with the nonsense you have to go through. I didn't want to fly, though.

"I'll drive," I said.

"The flight is less than two hours, sweetie."

"It's okay. I want to drive." I wanted my gun. I couldn't tell you why exactly. Maybe because I was in a mean mood, but I definitely wanted it with me. It's just about impossible to fly anymore with a gun.

"You sure?" she asked.

"Yeah. I can leave in a couple hours."

"So you'll be here in thirteen hours."

"Twelve," I said.

She laughed. "She wants to drive." I assume she was talking to Valerie.

"Figures," Valerie said in the background.

Figures? What the fuck did that mean? Like she knows me well enough to have an opinion. Valerie and I have a history, and it's not a good one.

"Where should I get a room?" I asked.

"Don't be silly," Rosa said. "You're staying here, sweetie."

"You sure it's cool?"

"Positive. It's cool."

"No one will shoot me in the head?"

She didn't laugh. It's not all that funny. The only reason I said it is because that was part of the bad history I have with Valerie. Yeah, the bitch shot me in the head a few years ago. It wasn't an accident either.

I didn't plan to stay long, so I didn't pack much. Before I left, I grabbed a couple thousand from the safe. It wasn't smart to put anything on the charge card. I didn't want Gretchen to find out that I'd gone to Miami. We have a joint credit card, but I'm the one who keeps track of the charges and pays it. That doesn't mean she doesn't know how to pull up the account on the computer. It'd be just like her to check up on me. Nope. I preferred Gretchen think that I was in Georgia and never know about Miami.

I packed up the car and typed Rosa's address into my GPS. "Please drive the highlighted route," the British-accented voice said.

"Are you out of your fucking mind?" should have been its response.

SIX

I had a lot of time to think while driving to Miami. It was probably a bad idea to leave Georgia. If Gretchen found out, she'd have a fucking fit, and there'd be no way we'd reconcile.

Although Gretchen has never met Rosa, she knows we're friends. She's tried to get me to say we were exes, but I never copped to it. I told Gretchen I've worked for Rosa, that she is my good friend who I've known since I was a kid, and I talk to her occasionally. That leaves out a lot. We've slept together, but technically aren't exes because we've never been a couple, even if in some ways we're more than a couple. It's complicated.

Meanwhile, I went through different scenarios in my head on how to get Gretchen to come back. Everything was transparent, pathetic. I wished Larry would feel sorry for me and admit his part in the whole fiasco. The biggest problem, of course, was that I did have sex with Mrs. Palmer, and she didn't put a gun to my head until afterwards. If I had it to do over again, I'd refuse her and let the consequences fall where they may. Gretchen is freaking incredible, and I'm a fucking idiot to jeopardize the relationship.

I've never been to Miami, though I was sent to Sarasota and Fort Lauderdale for hits.

Sarasota was a fucked up mess. My target was a blonde bimbo who threatened to spill the beans about an affair she was having with a well-known married football player. I was about an hour away from pulling the trigger when Rosa called and said it was off. They'd reconciled.

I ended up staying a few extra days because it was February, and I wasn't in a hurry to get back to Chicago. I hung out on the beach and let the heat seep into my bones. Rosa called again two days later and put the hit back on because the bitch pissed off the bastard again. Then, yep, you guessed it, Rosa called and said it was off for good. Rosa and I still made money.

The happy couple married, but it lasted less than a year. As far as I know, though, he didn't put out another hit on her. He remarried—sorry, ladies, he's taken.

The Fort Lauderdale job also got me away from a Chicago winter. It was Christmas, and I was sent to kill a gay guy who'd been blackmailing an actor. The movie star got tired of paying and worrying whether his ex would out him. This one was tricky because the target had a female roommate. She finally left for work, and the rest was easy.

I knocked on the door. He looked through the peephole, saw a girl, opened the door, whined, "Stacey's not here" and got shot in the forehead. He never saw the gun.

I ended up staying in Fort Lauderdale a few extra days because I met a woman in a dyke bar. She was a bartender and hot and a half. We had fun. I finally left when Rosa said I needed to come back for another job.

The funny thing is I absolutely cannot remember the woman's name. Every once in a while, I try to remember, and it's not there. Damndest thing. All I remember is she had a cross tattoo on her shoulder and told me she'd run away from home. I can't even remember where she'd run from. She was a sweet but troubled girl with a major drug problem. It wasn't difficult to leave her. I told her I'd call, but I didn't.

The drive from Atlanta to Miami was easy, virtually all interstate. Since it was Sunday morning, the traffic was light.

I quickly discovered that Miami is fucking hot. When I left Atlanta, the temperature was eighty. I glanced down at the car's thermometer when I exited off I-95, and it showed ninety-fucking-five.

Rosa's Crawford Avenue house was easy to find. A wave of wet, oppressive heat hit me when I stepped on her bricked driveway. The air was like a fucking greenhouse and staggered me for a second.

Once my eyes adjusted to the brightness, I glanced up at the house. It was a pretty one-story stucco with clay tiles on the roof. Large palms and grasses shielded much of it, and a short white wall surrounded the front yard. Large red flowers the size of dinner plates were planted in front of the stucco wall.

I peeked into the two-car garage and saw Rosa's green Jaguar. Unsure about the Valerie situation, I walked through the open iron gate onto the brick sidewalk and called Rosa to let her know I'd arrived. She shrieked with joy and ran out the front door, down the sidewalk, smiling, arms outstretched. I didn't see any sign of Valerie and figured she had better things to do than greet me.

The last time I saw Rosa was a few years ago when she dropped me off in Georgia after the California con. She hadn't changed. A few years had passed, but the familiar jolt of attraction smacked me. I think she felt something too.

"You look great," she said, adjusting her little white sun dress. "I was expecting a lot worse." Rosa gave me a hug, a quick kiss on the lips, and grabbed one of my backpacks.

Rosa never sweats. It was blazing hot on her shaded sidewalk, and perspiration poured off me. She didn't have a bead on her. She smelled good too. Something subtle, dark, and musky. Like if Axe had a cool lesbian sister.

I stepped inside, replaced my shades with my glasses, and

checked out the house. The interior had tons of large windows highlighting the cherry floors and high ceilings. They'd furnished it with Knoll.

Rosa led me to my room. "I'm impressed," I said, taking in the view of the pool through the floor-to-ceiling windows. French doors opened to the bricked patio.

"Believe me," she said proudly, "it didn't look like this when we bought it. We put a lot of work into it. It was built in the forties by a guy who owned a restaurant on the beach." She pointed to a large oak dresser near the window. "It's empty. Feel free to put your stuff in it. He kept marrying younger and younger. One of those. Got in trouble with the IRS and lost the house." Rosa waved at a closed door on the far wall. "That's your bathroom. The house was sold and then abandoned. A real estate guy bought it right before the bottom dropped out. It went into foreclosure. We got a great deal, but we've put tons of money into it."

Since moving to Miami, she and Valerie have been buying and selling real estate. Things have apparently gone well.

"Are you hungry?" she asked.

I wasn't. Still, I hadn't eaten since yesterday and figured I should get food in me. I shrugged.

"You're still vegetarian, right?" Rosa asked, while we walked to the kitchen.

I nodded. This was Gretchen's doing. I started living with her in California before she moved to Georgia to be with me. She was vegetarian, and I gradually evolved that way. It was more habit than anything, but I wasn't ready to give it up yet.

"I can scramble you some eggs," she said. "The way you like them." She meant with cream cheese and herbs.

"That'd be great. Now that's a stove," I said, when Rosa set a frying pan on the huge cobalt blue gas range.

"Valerie likes to cook," she said. "She knew exactly what she wanted. It's supposed to do something or other, but all I can do is cook eggs and grilled cheese. She's a whiz on it." Rosa cracked eggs into a bowl. "She can cook anything."

A few minutes later, Rosa sat me down on a steel bar stool at the black marble island. A plate of fluffy eggs, toast, and juice was in front of me. From behind, she put her arms around me, kissed the top of my head, and held the embrace for several moments. I let her.

"I'm glad you came, Kell," she said. "You've never been to Miami, have you?"

"No."

"I couldn't remember."

"Is Valerie around?"

"She went to see her aunt and uncle. We usually have breakfast with them at Nemo's on Sundays."

"You should have gone, Rosa."

"It's okay. I'll go next Sunday. She'll be back soon. Don't worry, Kell. It's cool. You haven't been sleeping." Rosa peered at my face. "How long have you been up?"

It hurt to think. "A long time."

"You should sleep after you eat. I'm jumping in the shower. Go ahead and eat and then I'll show you around. By that time, you'll be ready to crash."

She went off down the hall. While I was eating, the front door opened.

"Mrs. Kingsley," I said, when Valerie and I locked eyes. She looked tan, cool, and comfortable in a white sleeveless top and pants. Like Rosa, she hadn't changed much. The biggest change was she'd lightened her long brown hair.

"Lisa," she said.

We'd both used aliases when we met. She didn't smile or seem particularly happy to see me. Fine. The last time I'd seen her, she tried to kill me. Frankly, Valerie was lucky to be alive. As it was, I'd roughed her up.

"Did you have a nice trip?" she asked, just to have something to say.

"It was okay. It's too hot."

"It's Miami. Where's Rosa?" Valerie asked, already over the small talk.

"In the shower." I lowered my eyes, unable to think of a single thing to say to her. She apparently felt the same because she walked off to another room.

I ate and got sleepy, just like Rosa said I would. She gave me a brief tour of the house and then showed me to my room.

She pulled down the covers, and I slid into the bed, still fully clothed. Rosa pulled the covers up to my neck and sat on the edge of the mattress. She talked and talked until I turned her voice into a sound machine and fell hard asleep.

I slept a good long time and then took a shower and put on clean clothes. I found Rosa and Valerie lounging in the living room on the dark gray sofa with empty plates in front of them.

"Valerie made a pizza," Rosa said. "Help yourself to the leftovers in the fridge."

"You'll probably want to reheat it," Valerie said.

She got to her feet and took a few steps toward the kitchen, but I waved her off. "I got it."

I looked over my shoulder when I reached the kitchen to see if she'd followed. She hadn't.

I found the pizza and ate two pieces cold, standing up, eating like an animal. I thought it was delicious.

"We're hanging out in here, Kell," Rosa called out from the living room.

"Great pizza, Valerie," I said, joining them. "Thanks."

She smiled. "You're welcome." With Rosa in the room, Valerie was more gracious.

The lights were dim. A Bose stereo played Charlie Parker in the background. I slouched in a Barcelona chair with my feet on the matching ottoman. Rosa and Valerie faced me. Rosa had her legs tucked up underneath her. She wore another white sun dress. Sprawled on the couch, looking relaxed, Valerie had changed into blue jeans and a loose white shirt. Her bare feet touched Rosa.

They talked about renovating the house, dealing with contractors, and attending flea markets and auctions. They made me laugh with stories of boneheaded things they did during the construction. I'd gotten my second wind and enjoyed the conversation, especially since I'd been passed a joint and handed a cold Amber Bock.

"So," Rosa asked after a lull, "what happened between you and your girlfriend?"

I groaned and covered my face.

"Honey," Valerie said, nudging Rosa with her foot, "go turn down the system. I can't hear."

Rosa obediently got up and walked past me. I gave her a 'Well, you're certainly whipped, aren't you?' look. She pretended not to notice. She did notice, though, because on her way back, she cuffed my ear. I grinned and took another sip of beer.

"So she went to stay with your sister?" Rosa asked. "Is that analogous to going home to mother?"

"They've been friends a long time," I said. "My sister, Gin, is taking her side."

"What's her side?" Valerie asked.

"I sort of cheated on her, and she caught me," I said.

"Oh," they both said and nodded knowingly.

"I assume you've done the apologizing and begging," Rosa said.

"I didn't beg," I said.

"Maybe you should," Valerie said. She and Rosa shared a smile.

"I'm getting close," I said.

"Who'd you cheat with?" Rosa asked.

"That's the kick in the head. I was working something, and it wasn't even someone I wanted to do."

Valerie tilted her head back and giggled.

"You need to work on that excuse, sweetie," Rosa said.

I laughed. I was carried away by the weed and booze. I also liked looking at Rosa and Valerie. Both are knockouts, and I've had the pleasure of fucking both. I know what they're about, and what they're about is nice indeed. Valerie is Cuban and German and looks like a fucking model. I've always found Rosa attractive, even when she was my babysitter. Dark hair, dark eyes, great skin and body. There's a reason I usually end up in bed with her.

Valerie caressed Rosa with her toe. It was a turn-on. I felt guilty for thinking it, but you can't help what you think.

"Give her time," Rosa said.

"Maybe you two should plan a getaway," Valerie said.

Hadn't Larry suggested something like this too? My mind floated. I hadn't had much to drink, but Rosa's pot was stout. I felt good.

"I'll suggest it when she's speaking to me again," I said.

They softly laughed. I'd decided to head back to my room when Valerie sat up and kissed Rosa.

They went at it good. I probably should have left, but it was a damn good show. With the blizzard from Gretchen, I hadn't had sex in weeks since, well, Mrs. Palmer.

"Come here, Kell," Rosa said, after a few minutes, motioning for me. I hesitated a second, mainly to gauge Valerie's reaction. She dropped her mouth open and licked her lips. Rosa didn't have to ask twice. We fooled around some on the couch, and then went back to their bedroom.

I've had threesomes. In fact, I started doing it at such a young age that I thought I invented it. But a threesome with Rosa and Valerie made my head explode. This, I wasn't expecting. And on the first fucking night. Happy St. Lisa's Day. The last thing I remember was Valerie asking, "Is the alarm set?" I didn't hear Rosa's answer.

SEVEN

When I woke the next morning, Rosa and Valerie were out of bed and gone from the house.

I made my way to their huge fucking kitchen. The sun streamed through the windows, making the white kitchen even brighter. The coffee pot was turned off but still had coffee in it. I drank a cup. Stale, cold coffee was still coffee, and I'm an addict.

I found a note on the kitchen table. "Kell, we've gone to work. Help yourself to anything and everything. We'll be home sometime in the late afternoon. Call if you need anything." Rosa had written down her cell phone number, which I already knew, along with the codes for the front and back door locks and security system. It was signed Rosa & Valerie with a little heart and arrow. Cute.

I rubbed my face. Maybe last night was a blip. I could get used to it, but it probably wasn't something I needed to get used to. If Gretchen and I ever got back together, it would be tough explaining it.

After breakfast, I scoped out the house and changed into cutoffs and a tank top to sun myself by the pool. It turned out to be a bad idea. I didn't last more than half an hour because it was at least one hundred steamy degrees, and I was fucking miserable.

I came back inside and, believe it or not, got in the sauna. I know it seems counterintuitive, as they say, but the idea occurred to me, and I didn't regret it. The heat felt good and helped me relax. I came out after twenty minutes and then got on the laptop in the kitchen and checked my email. I had messages from Home Depot, Kim Komando, and a Nigerian woman named Mrs. Hope Criswell who was dying of cancer and wanted to give me a few million dollars. Nothing from Gretchen. I was disappointed but not surprised.

I snooped a bit on the Toshiba, but didn't get far. I couldn't get into the files without a password. All I could do was surf the Internet. I didn't care enough about the world to do that.

I wandered around the house and found a Nintendo Wii in the media room. I kicked ass at bowling until a car pulled up in the driveway. I peeked through the blinds. It was Valerie's Lexus.

She came in, carrying a black leather briefcase. Her hair was pulled back, and she wore a conservative gray pantsuit. Valerie was friendly, but we were awkward with each other.

"You and Rosa work in the same building?" I asked, not caring much, but feeling like someone needed to say something.

"Yes," she said. "We're in the Greene Building downtown. We have one entire floor. Of course, we're both out of the office a lot, looking at properties, meeting with people, you know."

I didn't know but smiled politely.

"What time does she usually get home?" I asked.

Valerie glanced at her watch. "Soon," she said. "She was scheduled to have a meeting. If she's late, she'll call."

"You guys happy in Miami?"

"Oh, yeah. It's a great city. Lots of opportunity. Especially now. You should think about moving here."

I have no desire to live in Miami. For one thing, it's too fucking hot. I might have been tempted if it were January or February, but it was fucking June.

"I'm happy in Georgia," I said.

She nodded. "It's nice there," she said.

This led to more awkwardness. The last time we'd seen each other was in Georgia. It hadn't gone well.

Valerie started to say something but stopped. She smiled tightly and then said, "Hey, I know it was a long time ago, but I'm sorry about what happened."

"Obviously," I said, not knowing what else to say.

"I'm glad you have a sense of humor about it. Rosa said you'd be okay, but I worried."

"It was a long time ago. We're in different places now."

"I want you to know that I *am* sorry."

"It's okay," I said. "Thanks."

Fortunately, Rosa arrived a few minutes later. We went out to a Mexican restaurant near the beach for dinner, and when we came back we ended up in the living room again. I wondered if I was in line for a second night of heaven. We talked about this, we talked about that, and, yep, we ended up in bed together. This time it started when Rosa changed the topic from something that happened on *Mad Men* to my body.

"You've gotten curvy, Kell," Rosa said. "Womanly. It becomes you."

Valerie nodded. "You've got a great body," she said.

Back in Chicago, when I was a regular hit man for Rosa, I worked out a lot and had a real hard body when I met Valerie. However, since being with Gretchen, I'd cut back on regular workouts. I was still in good shape. I often walked Thuggie several miles a day at the park, but I almost never went to the gym. Sometimes I played with Gretchen's Wii, but that was more her thing.

"Gretchen's a great cook," I said. This was true. She liked to cook, and, unlike when I was single, we had regular mealtimes. Gretchen also paid attention to nutrition and did a great job of getting me to eat better. "She's on me about cutting out junk and eating real food."

"I like the glasses too," Rosa said.

"They make you look smart," Valerie added.

"Older," I said.

"Come here, Kell," Rosa said, beckoning me to the sofa. "Show us your body." Maybe it was the pot, but I stood and slowly, once piece at a time, stripped. Rosa and Valerie watched until I got to my last piece, my white bikini panties.

Then they were on me. Doobie-doobie-do and all that. Yeah, I'd just been talking about how well Gretchen was taking care of me, but I'd have to be out of my fucking mind to turn this down. We went back to their bedroom, and I lost track of time.

"Is the alarm set?" Valerie asked, right before I fell asleep.

I didn't hear the alarm go off this time either. Someone—my guess was Rosa since she was closest—got to it quick. I also never heard them shower or dress for work. It was sweet of them, staying quiet, so I could sleep in.

This time, Rosa's note said the cleaning people would come around eleven. A marble guy and pool dude were expected in the afternoon. It was again signed with a little heart and arrow.

I spent most of the early morning writing a letter to Gretchen on the laptop. I doubted I'd send it, but it helped me organize my thoughts. Frankly, it was full of lies, but the gist of it was true. I wanted Gretchen back and would do just about anything.

I put away the flash drive and went for a swim. Although I hadn't swam in years, it was about the only sensible thing to do in Miami. The property was secluded, and since I didn't bring a bathing suit, I swam nude. I performed a few dives and half-hearted laps, but finally went back inside and got in the sauna. Rosa's place was like a fucking resort.

The cleaning brigade came and went. I'm not sure they had the necessary time to clean the house, but it looked clean enough to me, so who am I to say.

The pool dude never showed up, but the marble guy did. He

looked like a surfer and wore snug jeans and a white t-shirt so tight his nipples showed. He had white hair, was very tan, and wore several tattoos with ancient-looking symbols that didn't make any sense to me. One was on his forehead. He seemed pleasant but odd in more of a mental rather than a drug way.

I made small talk with him.

"So you're the marble guy," I said.

He flashed me a smile. "That's what they tell me," he said.

"What does a marble guy do?" I asked.

"I clean and repair it. I'm the best in Miami." He paused. "That's what the ladies say."

Not remotely in the mood to flirt, I excused myself and re-read the letter I'd written to Gretchen. Like I said, I didn't know if I'd ever show it to her, but it felt good having written it.

When Valerie returned at three-thirty, the marble guy was still in the house. Valerie carried in a paper plate with purple plastic wrapped around it. She set the plate on the kitchen table and expertly removed the wrap.

"Oatmeal peanut butter cookies," Valerie said.

Valerie offered some to the marble guy. The ill-mannered boor ate at least six. Valerie was at ease with him. They joked back and forth. He glanced at me several times. I crossed my arms and didn't speak. He finally left, and I ate one of the cookies.

"Homemade," I said.

"They're good. Aunt Marie made them. Uncle Buddy's wife." Valerie sighed. "She's in bad shape. She's diabetic and has heart trouble. I lived with them when I was younger. They don't have kids, so they unofficially adopted me. He's actually my dad's uncle. My parents split up. I wanted to stay in Miami, so they let me stay with them. He's the one who helped Rosa set up the business. I'm sure Rosa mentioned him."

Rosa hadn't mentioned him.

"He's been in real estate in Miami for decades," Valerie said.

"He knows everything there is to know. And everyone. Buddy Bach Properties. That's who he is."

"What do you guys do exactly?" I asked.

Valerie shrugged, not because she didn't know but because she didn't know how to explain it. "I look through newspapers and online listings for unique properties that seem to be a good deal. I research titles. Hire contractors to do the renovations. Things like that."

I nodded, but it still seemed vague to me.

"Rosa does the negotiations, of course," she said. "She keeps the books, runs the numbers, negotiates the terms, all that stuff."

"You like it?"

"Love it. Yeah. Every day is different. It doesn't get boring. It's competitive because other companies are doing the same thing. It might be something you'd enjoy."

I shook my head. "I don't think so."

"You're smart. It's challenging. I think you'd like it."

I didn't think I'd like it all, but there was no point arguing about it.

"What are you doing these days?" she asked.

"I work with my brother-in-law."

She waited for more. I didn't say anything. "What does he do?" she asked.

I smiled. "A little of this. A little of that."

"You don't want to tell me."

"It's hard to explain."

"Is it what you did with Rosa?"

"No."

"Scams?"

"Mm." I tilted my head back and forth.

"Aren't you afraid of getting caught?" she asked.

"Not really. You worried about me, Valerie?"

"It's none of my business, but maybe I am worried about you."

We were flirting, and we needed to stop.

Valerie realized it too. She cleared her throat and sat up straighter. "I still think you should consider moving here, maybe work for Rosa," she said.

I shrugged, surprised she was pushing so hard.

"It's all on the level?" I asked.

"Absolutely."

It occurred to me that maybe Valerie thought it was, but Rosa was working something. You never knew with her.

"We both decided after—" Valerie cut her eyes at me. "Uncle Buddy gave us a chance to do something different. He's a great guy. You need to meet him and Aunt Marie before you leave."

"You think you'll be doing this for a while?"

Valerie nodded. "The recession was the best thing that happened to us. This was one of the most overpriced markets in the country. There's tons of foreclosures."

"You didn't grow up in Atlanta?"

That's what she'd told me years ago.

She blushed. "No. I mostly grew up here."

"Didn't go to Emory?"

"No. I'm sorry—"

I waved her off. It was stupid to even bring it up. I'd been conned back then. Valerie and Rosa had worked it to perfection.

We heard Rosa's car door slam. That ended our conversation. I soon discovered that we were having dinner with Uncle Buddy and Aunt Marie at Quinn's. I hadn't brought anything dressy, so Rosa let me try on a couple of her dresses. We're not the same size, but close enough. I picked a little black one, and we piled into Rosa's green Jag and drove to the restaurant.

"Don't worry," Rosa said to me in the car. "They've got vegetarian dishes. I called and made sure."

That was sweet. Damned if I wasn't toying with the idea of moving to Miami. If I couldn't get Gretchen to move back, it might be a good idea to relocate. I could stay with Valerie and

Rosa before I found my own place. Or maybe I could live with them. On the one hand, it was dangerous to live in the same city with them. On the other hand, it might be a good deal, at least for a while.

Uncle Buddy and Aunt Marie were older than I'd imagined. Uncle Buddy was stooped and used a cane. Aunt Marie was in even worse shape. I don't suspect she was ever a tall woman, but now she was down to about four-foot-eight. She used a walker and moved excruciatingly slow, like someone in constant pain. They were expensively dressed, and I wondered how long it took to master that look of old money.

I ordered the spinach and ricotta ravioli. Everyone else ordered fish. Rosa chose a bottle of wine.

At one point, Rosa and Valerie told Aunt Marie about a building they'd bid on. They tried to explain where it was located which wasn't easy because Aunt Marie's hearing wasn't so hot.

Uncle Buddy turned his head and clasped my hand. "Did you know Rosa in Vegas?" he asked. His hand was cold. I could feel the bones in his fingers.

"No," I said. "Chicago."

I doubted Uncle Buddy knew much about Rosa's background, only what she'd told him. I wondered if he knew Valerie had been a prostitute in Vegas. He doted on his great niece, but Valerie probably hid much of her life from the family.

"Do you work in real estate too?" he asked.

"No," I said.

"What do you do, honey?" Aunt Marie asked, when the attention shifted to me.

"I'm a security consultant," I said. That's what Rosa and I came up with years ago. It was vague enough that no one asked additional questions. Usually.

"Oh," Aunt Marie said, sounding surprised.

"What's that?" Uncle Buddy asked.

"I look at residences and businesses and help people come up with a security package," I said.

Our food arrived. Rosa was attentive to Aunt Marie, even cutting her food for her. Valerie, too, hovered over her frail aunt.

"I might need your services," Uncle Buddy said to me during coffee. "How long will you be in town?"

I hesitated only a second. "I'm just here for a short visit," I said.

"Give me a call before you go. Is she here to do a security check on your house?" he asked Valerie.

Rosa answered. "No," she said. "She's working too hard in Atlanta and needed a break."

I don't know if anyone bought it. Aunt Marie smiled sweetly.

"Do you get that much work in Atlanta?" Uncle Buddy asked.

"I keep busy," I said.

"You should move to Miami," he said. "You could team up with us. When people buy a property, we could throw in a security analysis."

Again, someone was asking me to move to Miami. Maybe there was something to it.

"You've looked at Rosa's house, right?" Uncle Buddy asked.

I smiled.

"She's made suggestions," Rosa said. "It's ingrained in her. It's like us when we see a 'For Sale' sign, Uncle Buddy. We start thinking."

Aunt Marie nudged Valerie with a tiny fist she made with her left hand. Valerie was on her feet immediately, helping Aunt Marie to hers. With her other hand, Valerie grabbed the large pink canvas satchel she'd brought into the restaurant. "We'll be right back," she said.

Rosa stood. "You need some help?" she whispered to Valerie.

"I'll go," I said, knowing I didn't want to be stuck alone with Uncle Buddy. I stood and clutched Aunt Marie's other tiny arm.

Rosa and Valerie exchanged glances.

"I need to use the restroom anyway," I said.

Rosa sat down, and Valerie and I led Aunt Marie to the bathroom. Once in the bathroom, Valerie guided Aunt Marie into a stall. I went into the adjoining stall and peed, flushed, and then came out and washed my hands. The other stall door was still closed. I leaned against the sink and folded my arms.

"Kell." It was Valerie's voice.

"Yeah."

"Could you do me a favor?"

"Sure."

"The bag I brought in—" I glanced over at the pink satchel on the counter.

"Yeah."

"Could you please bring it to me?"

I grabbed the satchel, and Valerie unlatched the stall door. I peered in. Valerie, in front of Aunt Marie, was holding an adult diaper, folded several times. Behind Valerie, Aunt Marie awkwardly squatted, gripping the grab bar. Her eyes were closed, and her head slumped to the side.

"Could you please throw this in the garbage?" Valerie asked. "You'll be fine if you hold it like this," she added and demonstrated, keeping it flat and unmoving.

I took the diaper, and Valerie rifled through the bag and pulled out a clean diaper. She expertly secured it to Aunt Marie.

I stepped away and threw away the soiled diaper while Valerie led Aunt Marie, now wide awake, out of the stall. We washed her hands and then our own. Finally, we walked Aunt Marie back to the table.

Rosa shot me a look of thanks when I sat. I nodded. Aunt Marie squeezed Valerie's hand, and then mine.

"Everything okay?" Uncle Buddy asked. His tone indicated that he knew it was, but wanted to acknowledge the kindness shown.

"Perfect," Valerie said.

Uncle Buddy insisted on paying. Rosa argued with him, but Uncle Buddy whispered something in her ear. She smiled and nodded her head.

"Will I really have to do a security check on his house?" I asked, when we were back in Rosa's car. In fact, I did know how to do such a thing. I'd often made sure houses and businesses were secure when I was a bodyguard. I'd also kept up with the new technology and could fake it if I needed to. I just didn't find the work all that interesting.

"No," Rosa said. "He's like that. He wants to help you."

I thought she'd follow up by telling me it would be a good idea to move to Miami, but Valerie talked about how weak Aunt Marie seemed. They ended up in a discussion about whether they should have a home health service visit a couple times a week.

"What did Uncle Buddy say to you?" Valerie asked. "At the end of the meal, when you two argued over who would pay."

"He said he wouldn't have lots of opportunities to buy me a good meal. To shut up and let him do something nice for me."

"He's been on that kick for a while," Valerie said. "Maybe the doctor said something to him."

"Is he sick?" I asked.

"He's not in great health," Valerie said. "Hasn't been for a while."

"He's had some lapses too," Rosa said. "Don't get me wrong. He's still real sharp, but there have been a few times he's made mistakes. Poor guy. He took it hard." She paused. "It'll happen to all of us eventually. If we live long enough."

EIGHT

Back at Rosa's, I went to my room and changed my clothes. Rosa and Valerie were moving around, and I figured they were getting ready for bed. Neither are big drinkers, but they'd had some wine at the restaurant and were probably tired. It also occurred to me that they might want to spend some time with each other. We'd gone at it two nights in a row. Maybe they needed a break.

Rosa eventually strolled through my open doorway, holding a joint. She sat on the bed, and we passed the joint back and forth.

"I'm glad you came down here," she said.

"I am too. I would have been miserable in Georgia."

"You still haven't heard from her?"

"No."

"Poor baby. You could call her."

"She asked me not to."

"Yeah," Rosa said, "but it might be a test. She might really want you to call her."

"I'd prefer she call me."

"She's crazy not to."

"Thanks, Rosa."

"Got a picture of her?" she asked.

"Of course." I grabbed my phone from the nightstand and tapped to the photos. "That's Thuggie," I said, showing Rosa a shot of the dog.

"Aw, he's cute."

"He's a good boy. I miss him."

I showed her a picture of Bella. Rosa's eyes widened. "Jeez," she said. Bella really is a behemoth.

I clicked on a photo of Gretchen. She was in the kitchen cooking on the stove. I'd called out her name, and she'd turned her head. Her eyebrows were raised as though she were saying, "Huh?"

"She's beautiful," Rosa said. "But I can tell she won't let you get away with anything."

I tapped on another photo. It was Gretchen and Gin back in Oceanvue. They were sitting on the beach in shorts and sunglasses smiling at the camera, shielding their eyes.

"Your sister," Rosa said.

"Yep."

I put down the phone. Rosa kissed me. I kissed her back. She stood. "Coming back with us tonight?"

Rosa, Valerie, and I quickly got in a routine. I wasn't over Gretchen. However, Rosa and Valerie's attempt at sexual healing, or whatever the hell they were doing, didn't make me feel worse. Maybe I'd stay awhile. Then I could make a decision about moving to Miami permanently.

It worked out for them too. I supervised the steady stream of workers who came to the house. In the past, one of them had to leave work or give out the security code and then change it. This was a better solution.

I was also recruited to drop things off at their office. The Greene Building was located a few miles from the house in a shimmering glass high-rise. I learned the name of their company—Gold-Bach Enterprises LLC—and got better acquainted with Uncle Buddy. He was quite a character and struck me as a sharp cookie. Considering he used a cane, he got around well. Five feet tall and in his eighties, he always wore a fresh flower in his suit lapel and had impeccable manners. Rosa and Valerie adored the dapper little dude.

Almost two weeks had passed, and I still hadn't heard from Gretchen. "Don't bury her yet," Rosa told me, but I was beginning to wonder. I even Googled her name to see if anything new came up. It didn't. I also checked to see if she'd joined Facebook. She hadn't. She hates those kinds of things, but I wondered if she might reconsider now that she was kind of single.

I was beginning to accept that she might be gone for good and asked Rosa if I could hang out with her at work to get a better idea of what she did.

"You should hang out with Valerie," she said. "My day is usually meetings and accounting programs. Dry. Not very glamorous."

I looked at Valerie. "I don't mind. It'll be fun," she said.

The next day I rode to work with Valerie. I hadn't brought anything to Miami other than jeans and t-shirts, so I wore newer jeans with a white linen shirt borrowed from Valerie and a brown blazer from Rosa. My long hair was pulled back in a barrette. Before we went in, Valerie and Rosa fussed over me, putting on make-up, dolling me up big-time. I even wore pearl earrings and a necklace.

Valerie and I got in at eight and spent the first half hour or so drinking coffee with Uncle Buddy.

"Are you here to do a security check on the building?" he asked.

"We're showing her what we do on a daily basis," Valerie said.

"We'll hire you yet, Kelly," Uncle Buddy said. He couldn't get my name right. No one calls me Kelly. My real name is Kelleher.

Most people call me Kell. Some old people just can't compute my name.

"It might happen," Valerie said.

"We've already got some video cameras up," he said, thinking. "There's a doorman. You have to sign in."

"Adam, John, and the temps don't do anything but look at girls," Valerie said.

Uncle Buddy shrugged. "From what you've seen," he asked, "do you think we need more security?"

I wasn't expecting this. Valerie didn't jump in to help. I needed to sound like an expert. "The doorman and video are deterrents, but if someone is serious it won't stop them," I said.

He blinked and took another sip of coffee.

"I'd suggest an armed security guard on the floor," I said. "Plain clothes. Someone trained as a bodyguard. Of course, most people don't want the extra expense. I'm not sure you need this. Have there been any problems?"

"Not that I'm aware of," Uncle Buddy said.

"Anyone in the building had security issues?" I asked.

He looked at Valerie. She shrugged.

"I guess what you're saying," he said, "is that we have sufficient security for our needs."

"I'd do some research and see if you need heightened security," I said. "If you don't, then, yes, you should be okay. Are the cameras twenty-four-seven?"

"I have no idea. Valerie?" Uncle Buddy asked.

"My understanding is that they run all the time," Valerie said. "I don't know about weekends. I'd have to ask."

"What happens to the feed?" I asked. "Is it archived?"

Valerie and Buddy shrugged.

"You impressed him," Valerie said, after we went back to her office. "He'll offer you a job. He might hire you through his company. We're actually two companies. The one he owns with Rosa and the one he had before we moved here. His offices are down one floor."

I'm not business-oriented and have little interest in it. I didn't see much difference between the two companies, but it seemed an important distinction to Valerie.

I had already been introduced to the receptionist, Dolores Rubio. She was fine. No wonder Rosa hired her. Dolores had long dark hair and looked young, but I can't judge age anymore. She dressed conservatively but had some nice assets. Charming smile too. She handed Valerie a stack of phone messages.

"How'd you do on that biology test?" Valerie asked Dolores.

Lordy, I hoped she wasn't in high school.

"92," Dolores said.

"Where do you go?" I asked. She had to be in college.

"University of Miami," she said.

"Cool. What are you studying?" I felt old.

"She's pre-med," Valerie said.

I wouldn't have minded hanging out with Dolores, but she was busy with the phones. Noticing she spoke Spanish with some callers, I figured that came in handy in Miami.

I went off with Valerie. She walked me down one floor to introduce me to Ray Regina, the company attorney. He had an office near the end of a long hallway. Like Uncle Buddy, he was ancient.

"He and Uncle Buddy are bocce buddies," Valerie said.

I shrugged. "I don't know what that is," I said.

Valerie looked to Ray to explain it to me. "It's the Italian version of bowling," he said.

I didn't like something about him. It'd surprise me if he was Rosa's hire. Must be Uncle Buddy's. I hate to stereotype, but the dude seemed Sopranoish. He was obese with slick, sparse gray hair combed straight back. I smiled and nodded. As it was, I doubted he'd get anything by Rosa. She could take care of herself, but he still didn't feel right.

Valerie spent the rest of the morning showing me how she

used computer databases and newspapers to find new property listings. When she found something potentially interesting, she researched it further. I could see how the hunt might be fun. I just couldn't see doing it every day.

Later that morning, she introduced me to Dana Brent, the student intern. Her hours varied, so she hadn't been around when I'd stopped in before.

Dana was a fucking knockout. One of those women who make you flush inside. She had medium-length brown hair and a husky voice. She was like if Jodie Foster and Johnny Depp hooked up and had a baby.

I smiled. She smiled back.

"So what does she do for you?" I asked Valerie, when we returned to her office. It might sound like I was being suggestive, but I swear I wasn't. Valerie was professional in everything she did and said, and I tried to do the same.

"She runs errands," Valerie said. "Does the photocopying. Proofing. Some research. Writing. Anything that comes up. She's great. Smart. Personable. We got lucky with her. She's a gem. Anything we've given her, she's exceeded our expectations."

"Uh-huh."

"She keeps hinting that she wants us to hire her full-time after the internship. We might. Especially if you decide to go back to Georgia. In some ways, she reminds me of Rosa."

I didn't see it. "How so?" I asked.

"She's ambitious. That can be a double-edged sword though." Valerie wanted to say more but decided not to. We got back to work.

About an hour later Valerie, left to use the restroom. Dana popped her head in.

"Hey," she said.

"Hey."

"Where's Valerie?" she asked.

"Ladies room."

She nodded. Dana was half in and half out of the office, hanging on the doorframe.

"Do you work here now?" she asked.

I shook my head. "No. I'm just hanging out. I'm Rosa's friend. I live in Georgia. Are you a student?"

"Yes."

"What are you studying?"

"Finance with a minor in real estate." Dana looked over her shoulder and turned back to me. "At Florida Atlantic. I'm hoping they'll hire me here."

I got it. I put up my hands. "I'm just hanging out with them," I said. "I'm not looking to work here."

We smiled. I got the idea we were thinking the same thing.

"They're great people to work for," she said. "I can't say enough about them. I've learned so much. It's been an incredible opportunity." She *was* ambitious. She thought I had pull. I gave her a look that let her know I was on to her. She laughed and briefly covered her face. When she uncovered it, her face was pink. She was adorable, but, yes, probably too young.

"I'll do what I can," I said.

"I'd appreciate it."

She glanced down the hall and straightened up. Valerie was on her way back.

"Valerie, I'm going down to the tax office," Dana said. "Do you need me to do anything before I go?"

"Did you finish proofing Rosa's PowerPoint?" Valerie asked.

"Yep," Dana said. "It's ready to go."

"Great. No, that's all. I'll see you tomorrow."

Valerie made a few phone calls, and then we met Rosa for lunch at the Lime Fresh Mexican Grill. After lunch, Valerie and I spent the rest of the afternoon looking at properties that she'd researched that morning. We also stopped by a four-story building on Third Street to check on its progress with the contractor. Valerie took notes on her laptop and called Rosa a couple times to confer. All in all, it was mildly interesting. I could see myself doing it for maybe a year.

My mind went back to Dolores and Dana. If Valerie dragged me back to the office again, I'd come up with a way to get to know them better, especially Dana. The thought started out good in my head but ended with guilty pangs in my chest. Gretchen was surrounded by pretty college students, and she was able to control herself. She'd never given me a reason to feel threatened or jealous. It made me miss her even more.

That night I tried to explain to Rosa and Valerie why I didn't think it was a good idea to hire me. They wanted me to take over Valerie's job, and then have Rosa train her to do some of her stuff with the idea that Rosa would open up a branch somewhere else. Something like that. I wasn't paying a lot of attention because, like I said, business is boring to me.

"Maybe you should hire Dana," I said. "She's got the background. You already like her, and—"

"Dana's great," Rosa said.

"She's wonderful," Valerie agreed.

"But," Rosa said, "I'd rather bring in someone I trust."

"You don't trust her?" I asked.

Rosa shrugged. "Not like I trust you. She's an unknown. I'd prefer to keep it in the family."

"Dana will learn what she can and then start her own company." Valerie shrugged. "I don't know. Maybe that's the type we need. We haven't figured it out yet."

"She impressed me," I said. I could stop now. I'd given Dana a good shot.

"Me too," Rosa said. "Believe me, we're thinking about it. Still, you're a known commodity. That's huge."

The conversation went here and there until Rosa said, "There's this one guy who's making life difficult for us."

I was buzzed and only half-listening. They'd been talking

about the business for so long that I was thinking it was time to head back to the bedroom.

"Who is he?" I asked, just to say something.

"Another real estate guy," Rosa said. "It's like he shadows us, knows what we're doing. He outbids us on properties and scoops things up before we finalize. It's damn frustrating."

"I can see that," I said.

"He's a dick," Valerie said. "He doesn't play fair."

"Uh-huh."

"He's killed us on some deals," Rosa said. "Cost us hundreds of thousands, I'd guess."

"Wow," I said.

"It's just a matter of time before someone takes him out," Rosa said.

Oh. Valerie said something about seeing him in an expensive restaurant with a plastic-surgery bimbo who was half his age. It sent us off on a conversation about how none of us found fake boobs attractive, and what was it about guys that they did. Of course, one thing led to another.

Before I fell asleep, my mind wandered back to the nameless investor who was making problems for Rosa and Valerie. He troubled me, and I don't like being troubled. I decided I'd change the subject if he came up again.

NINE

The next day was Friday. I stayed home because the marble guy, the rescheduled pool dude, and the tile dyke were expected. Neither the marble guy nor pool dude showed up, but the tile dyke did.

Rosa had told me she was cute and said she was worried we'd run away together. Rosa sometimes has a weird sense of humor, so I wasn't sure what to expect.

"Risa Rispoli of Rispoli Tile and Stone," said the cute brunette at the door.

"Kell."

"Nice to meet you. I'm here to inspect the bathrooms."

She seemed in a hurry, so I let her in and left her alone while she hustled through the house.

"Excuse me," she called out from the top of the stairs thirty minutes later.

Surfing the web in the kitchen, I looked up from the laptop.

"This house has four bathrooms, right?" she asked.

Risa was looking for an excuse to talk. "I think so," I said. "I don't live here." I included enough pauses in the two sentences to let her know that I knew she knew the number of bathrooms.

"I don't think I've seen you here before," she said sheepishly.

"Think or know?"

She laughed. I did too.

Risa reminded me of Gretchen. If Gretchen were Italian, short, and wore white coveralls. They laughed the same and had intelligent, sparkly brown eyes. You could almost see what was going on inside their clever brains.

"You staying long?" she asked.

"I don't know. I'm going through a breakup. I live in Georgia."

"Ah," she said. The "Ah" should have come after the second sentence, but it took Risa a moment to decide whether my recent breakup was a deal breaker. Apparently it was because she lost the smile and quickly left for another appointment. Still, I made a mental note to talk to her again if I was still in Miami the next time she returned to the house.

That night Rosa, Valerie, and I went to a great Indian restaurant named Ishq. I got a vegetable curry, and Rosa and Valerie ordered chicken dishes. I don't usually drink much, but Rosa convinced me to try a rum drink called Lakshmana. It was powerful. By the time we left, I was pre-hammered.

The real estate guy came up again later that night when we were in bed. "The guy we were talking about," Rosa said, "screwed us again today. Valerie found a property. When we made an offer, we found out it was already under contract. God, that guy pisses me off."

"How bad is he hurting you?" I asked. I'm not sure why I asked. It was like I was a fucking puppet, and someone pulled my string.

"He got the property for a little less than a quarter million," Rosa said. "After he does his thing, he'll probably sell it for a million."

"Wow. How is he so good at it?" I asked.

"He bribes people," Rosa said. "At least that's what we're guessing."

"We've even wondered if he's hacking into our emails,"

Valerie said. "Martinez does it to everyone. Not just us. It's maddening."

The dude had a name now.

"We've thought he might use women as bribes," Rosa said.

"Someone will eventually get fed up," I said.

The room grew quiet.

"You would think," Rosa said.

"What's his schedule?" I asked.

Rosa leaned forward. "Very predictable. He practically lives at his office. He's cheap. Got all kinds of money but keeps his office in a shabby part of town. He only has a part-time assistant who comes in twice a week. Everything else is farmed out."

Thinking I'd already said too much, I didn't say anything else. Rosa and Valerie were good to me that night. Like I said, it was a Friday night, so we had some fun.

Afterwards, Rosa brought smoked Gouda, sliced apples, and French bread back to the bed. "You know," I said, "if you guys want, I can take care of that guy for you."

They avoided looking at each other. "I don't know," Rosa said. Valerie stayed quiet.

"It's up to you," I said, licking apple juice off my fingers. "I'm just saying."

"I thought you were getting out of that line of work." Rosa offered me an out. Maybe she felt guilty.

"If you think it'd help, I don't have a problem with it," I said. I was saying it but hoped she'd say no. In truth, I hadn't pulled a hit in years. In fact, the last one was when I was with Valerie. I rarely went to the range anymore. After Gretchen moved in, I pretty much stopped because I didn't want her asking questions. I sometimes snuck in a few rounds, just to see if I could still shoot. I could, but I wasn't in the same league I was in when I worked for Rosa in Chicago. For God's sake, I even wore glasses now.

I was bragging, showing off in front of them. Maybe part of me wanted to please them, flatter them, let them know I'd do what they asked. Even so, I had qualms about the job, despite what I was saying out loud.

We didn't talk any more about it that night. I hoped it'd be forgotten, but the next morning at breakfast Rosa was all business.

"Kell," Rosa said, "his office is on the second floor of a storefront. There's no doorman, no video, no security. There's on-street parking, but there's also a parking lot about half a block away that might be a better place. He's there on Saturdays. He's alone. No assistants. There are three sections of stairs."

"Three flights?" I asked.

"No," she said. "Not flights." Rosa demonstrated with her hand how the stairs were constructed. "About five steps each." I nodded. "You get to the top. His office is to your left. All the other offices up there are vacant. His door is smoked glass. It'll be open if he's there. His desk is right inside. About five feet away from the door, facing it. Most likely, he'll be at his desk. His office is small."

"Does he have a gun?" I asked.

"I have no idea," Rosa said. "If he does, he'll see you, a pretty girl. Bam."

Valerie had made eggs and fried potatoes. I'd put down my fork when Rosa started talking. Now I picked up the fork and continued eating. Wow, I thought, I'm in it now.

"He drives a vintage T-bird," Rosa said. "It's always parked outside. It's red. The license plate is LM 4028. If it's there, he's there. He doesn't drive anything else."

Valerie didn't participate in the conversation. She was nervous. Averting her eyes, hands shaking, the whole bit. She should be. I mean, we're talking about killing a man here. Any normal person would find it disconcerting. I guess that means Rosa and I aren't normal.

Rosa and I had a successful contract-killing thing for a while.

Anyway, it was a long time ago. And here we are, though we agreed years ago we wouldn't do this anymore. I guess old habits creep back if you're stressed enough. She felt this guy was cheating her out of oodles of money. It made her nuts. I was out of sorts because Gretchen left me. It made me crazy. That's a recipe for something.

She didn't say it, but Rosa wanted me to do the hit today. Fine. Better sooner than later. Once I'm assigned a project, I like to get it over with.

"Name your price," Rosa said.

I don't need money. Back when things went bad between Rosa and me, I ended up taking quite a bit of her money. Payback and all.

"You're sure he doesn't have a bodyguard or security?" I asked. It surprised me because rich people usually do.

Valerie took her plate to the counter. She hadn't eaten much.

"He's too cheap," Rosa said, glancing at Valerie. "He does everything low budget. There's no way he'd hire security."

It was confession time. "Just so you know, Rosa," I said.

Valerie listened too. She was at the counter, now methodically scrubbing out the frying pan.

"I haven't been at a firing range in a while," I said. "The last time I did anything like this was in Atlanta when you sent me. I'm telling you this, so you'll know there might be a better person out there."

"This isn't complicated," Rosa said. "It's a piece of cake. If I didn't think you could do it, I wouldn't ask. I want you to know, though, if it doesn't feel right, don't do it."

Valerie shifted her feet. Her hand kept up the rhythmic, circular scrubbing.

"You brought your gun, didn't you?" Rosa asked.

She knew me well. "Yes," I said.

"Let me show you what he looks like." Rosa brought her laptop to the table, booted it up, and clicked around. She turned the laptop, so I could see the screen. Herb Martinez was a middle-aged guy. Balding, big nose, little mouth, brown eyes, and a mole on his left cheek.

"Got it," I said after a few moments.

Back in the day, Rosa and I would have been much more professional. This felt amateurish, rushed, half-assed. Maybe it ultimately didn't make much difference, but I wondered if we were making a big mistake by winging this thing. Rosa didn't seem concerned. In the past, she was the one obsessed with every detail. Everything was always worked out to the nth degree.

This particular hit was her thing. If it didn't bother her, I guess it shouldn't bother me.

TEN

We skinny-dipped in the pool after breakfast, but Rosa and Valerie were tense, distracted. After about a half hour, I asked, "You think he's there now?"

Rosa nodded. I got out of the pool, dressed, and left the house with my gun. I plugged Martinez's address into my GPS and started driving.

Martinez's building wasn't in a ghetto, but it wasn't suburbia either. Let's call it slumburbia. Gang graffiti defaced fences. Abandoned grocery carts were trashed in the weeds of overgrown lots. Fast food wrappers littered yards and roads. Eerie, vacant strip malls oozed failure. Depressing. Or maybe that was my mood.

I didn't see the T-bird on my first pass. I gunned the Mustang around the block and drove by again. This time I slowed, but the red car wasn't there. Rosa would be disappointed. So was I. You get keyed up over something like this. When it doesn't happen, you want to bang your head with your fists.

I parked in the lot that Rosa had recommended and cleaned out my glove compartment. I found a couple coupons for Pizza Hut. I crumpled them along with expired coupons for a Mexican restaurant and a car wash. Gretchen was big on using coupons.

I climbed out of the car, tossed everything in the nearest garbage can, took a couple steps and then got paranoid, envisioning an enterprising cop searching through all the garbage cans. Once a paranoid thought enters your head, it owns you. Atlanta coupons would tie me to the murder scene. I reached into the garbage can, pulled out the crap I'd thrown in, and shoved the expired coupons in my back pocket.

I walked through a small brick plaza with concrete benches. After that, I crossed the street and continued on the sidewalk. The T-bird still hadn't shown up.

Several cars sped by, and the few pedestrians were walking fast, minding their own business. Rosa had picked a good day. But only if the dude showed up. I went back to my car.

I turned on the radio but couldn't take listening to music. Pop music is all about love. That's the last thing I wanted to hear because love songs make me think of Gretchen, and I didn't want to think about her. I searched through the stations until I found a talk station. I could only take it for a few minutes because the host and the callers were fucking stupid. It was mainly anti-Obama and anti-woman. The comments were rude and sophomoric. Fucking hateful too. Gretchen taught me that you could have different political beliefs and still be civil. She was a huge fucking liberal but had plenty of friends who were Republicans. She explained that she'd grown up in a divided house. "If they can work it out, then everyone else can," she'd said more than once.

I flipped around some more until I found a PBS station playing classical music. I left it there, closed my eyes, and zoned out. I tried to think of nothing and succeeded until the music—I think it was Vaughn Williams—ended. An interview began with an author who'd written a book on anticipation. She explained that for most people it was the anticipation of the thing, rather than the thing, that gave them the most pleasure. I'd studied psychology a few years ago and came close to getting my masters, so this was up my alley. I wondered about the theory and my job as a hit man. The excitement, if you want to call it that, is in the planning and everything that leads up to the hit. Usually, the hit is anticlimactic.

I looked at the car clock and realized that more than an hour had passed since I'd first arrived. I got out of the car and repeated my earlier steps. Still no sign of the T-bird. I figured that Rosa might be worried, so I strolled back to my car, drove around the block one last time, and headed back to her place.

Rosa looked at me expectantly when I walked in. Valerie stood awkwardly at an angle and nervously rubbed her hands together. I didn't get the feeling that she was totally on board with this.

"His car wasn't there," I said.

Rosa wasn't happy. "What do you mean, it wasn't there?"

"I looked for the red T-bird. It wasn't there."

"What took you so long?" she asked.

"I waited to see if he'd show up," I said.

She tried not to be pissed off, but was. It wasn't my fault, of course, but she wanted it over. I understood and didn't hold it against her.

"I'll try again another day," I said. "It's cool, Rosa."

"He's always there," she said. "The guy lives in his office."

I shrugged.

"Fuck," she said, under her breath.

"Maybe—" Valerie started to say, but didn't finish her statement.

"You know what a T-bird looks like, right?" Rosa asked.

I gave her a look. She got the message.

Everyone was tightly wound, so we headed off in different directions. I'm not sure where Valerie and Rosa went. I went into the kitchen, sat at the island, and checked my emails on the laptop. Same old crap and nothing from Gretchen.

A phone rang. A few minutes later, someone thudded down

the hall. Shortly after that, the front door opened and closed.

"Kell."

Rosa stood in the doorway with her arms crossed.

"Did Valerie leave?" I asked.

She nodded. "Uncle Buddy's in the hospital."

"What happened?"

"We're not sure. It might be a heart attack. Valerie has to pick up Aunt Marie and take her to the hospital. He was at his club when something happened. An ambulance came."

"Will he be okay?"

"She'll call when she finds out more."

"Is he conscious?"

"We don't know. We just know he collapsed. An ambulance was called."

"That's terrible."

Rosa nodded. "He's not in great health. This isn't totally unexpected." She moved closer and looked at the computer screen. "He's been a great help to me. I'm not sure if I—" Her voice faded.

"It'll be okay."

"Yeah. We'll deal with it. He knows so much more than me. It's a jungle out there. I don't know what I'll do." It was rare for Rosa to express lack of confidence. This was hitting her hard.

"Don't bury him yet, Rosa."

She faintly smiled. "They're like Valerie's parents. Her real dad is okay but not around much. Her mom—" Rosa shook her head. "She's a trip but not one you want to take. They don't get along. Her brother and sister are a lot older. They're not close. Valerie was a surprise. Her mom didn't want to raise her. Her parents split up when she was in high school. That's why she moved in with Uncle Buddy and Aunt Marie. Her mom went to California. Her dad went to England." She sighed. "Do you mind going back to Martinez's to see if he's there yet?"

Damn, she was in a hurry to get this done.

"No problem."

"Remember," Rosa said, before I left, "if you feel something's not right, walk away from it." Her voice broke. It embarrassed her. "I can't have something happen to you and Uncle Buddy all at the same time."

"I'll be fine." I kissed her. Rosa grabbed me, kissed me hard, and felt me up.

"Don't let anything happen to you," she said, sending me out with a shove.

ELEVEN

The red T-bird was on the street. I drove to the lot, parked my car, and walked across the plaza.

My phone rang. It should have been turned off. I was out of practice with this whole hit man thing. I used to be so fucking professional. I mean, leave my fucking phone on? That was peewee league.

I glanced down and saw the number. It was Gretchen. I hesitated only a second before answering. Yeah, it was unprofessional. I should have finished the job before taking a call, but I wanted to hear what she had to say. I was dying to hear her voice. At least I thought I was.

"Hello." I sat on a concrete bench and eyed the street ahead.

"Kell."

"Yeah."

"You doing okay?" Gretchen asked. Her voice was funny.

"Yeah."

"You got a minute?"

"Uh, I'm actually—" I certainly couldn't tell her I was in the middle of a hit. "What's up?"

"I wanted to talk to you."

"Uh-huh."

"I'm still thinking things over, but I need to tell you something."

I had a good idea what was coming next and wished I hadn't answered the fucking phone.

"I've starting casually dating," Gretchen said.

I stayed quiet. I wouldn't make it easy for her.

"Are you there?" she asked.

"Yeah. I'm here." She obviously pictured me in Georgia. Let's face it, she wouldn't have called if she knew I was in Miami, fucking Rosa and Valerie, and carrying out hits.

"It's not serious or anything like that," she said, "but I didn't think it was fair not to tell you."

"Okay," I said, sounding emotionless. Meanwhile, I wanted to box my own head for answering the fucking call right before the fucking hit. I am a fucking moron.

"You're okay with it?" she asked.

"I have to be, don't I?"

Gretchen sighed. "It's not easy being away from you."

I needed to get my fucking wits about me.

"If you want to go out with other people, go out," I said. "I want you to be happy. Hey, I'm not trying to be rude, but I was in the middle of something when you called. Is it okay if I call you back later?"

This rattled her. "No," she said firmly, "you don't have to call back. I just wanted you to know."

"That you're seeing other people."

"I'm casually dating."

"Okay. You've done your duty."

That steamed her. "At least I tell you before I fuck someone—never mind."

"Do you want me to call back or not?" I was acting like a punk. Like an immature little bitch who's just realized the world isn't fair and then keys someone's car.

"No." She hung up.

That went well. I turned off the fucking phone and headed toward Martinez's office, begging myself to fucking focus. I wondered why she'd called. Maybe she was weakening. Of course, if she was, I'd done my best to stiffen her resolve. Fuck me.

Upon reaching the brick building, I glanced at the T-bird and then used a tissue to open the wooden front door. I walked inside.

I have an advantage as a hit man. I'm a girl. No one suspects me for a moment. I'm just a girl wearing shades, dressed in a plain white t-shirt and blue jeans. It's not like I'm invisible because I get plenty of looks, but the bizarre thing is that when witnesses are asked if they saw anyone in the vicinity of the hit, they never mention me. They see me, but they don't *say* they saw me. I don't get it, but I use it. If I don't act suspicious, I can get away with murder.

The tiny foyer led to a closed jewelry store on my right and five worn wood stairs on my left. I quietly climbed the stairs in my Chuck Taylor's and felt for my gun. It was in a black nylon purse thing hooked to my belt loop.

The building was low-rent. Rosa would never have an office in a place like this. I might, but it wouldn't do for someone like Rosa. Don't get me wrong. I can't stand cheap. But this place had an old-time feel that made me comfortable. It was retro like a detective's office in an old Hollywood movie. The stairs were warped from thousands of feet. The plaster walls were rough to the touch. The place smelled old but not in a bad way. More like a subtle scent of pipe tobacco and old wood. There were lots of buildings in Chicago like this one. It made me nostalgic.

I continued climbing the stairs. When I reached the top landing, I stopped and listened but heard nothing. Martinez's office was a few feet ahead on my left. The door was open, just like Rosa said. It always takes a bit of nerve to confront the target. For all I knew, he was sitting at his desk holding a bazooka ready to blow a huge hole in me. I had my hand on the gun, but hadn't pulled it out.

I hesitated briefly and then stepped into the doorway. Martinez was at his desk holding a pen in his right hand. He appeared to be writing something on his desk calendar.

This turned out to be the easiest hit I've ever had. Someone beat me to it. Dude was already dead.

Martinez's head was turned to the side and lying on the desk, facing the wall. From the looks of it, he'd been shot point blank twice in the forehead. It wasn't pretty, but I stared.

Feeling vulnerable standing out in the hall, I stepped into his office. Hell, there was a murderer loose. I glanced around the office. The pipe tobacco I smelled? Dude was a smoker. He had a humidor on his desk next to his computer. A pipe rested on his desk calendar. Loose tobacco spread over the desk. There were coffee stains on the calendar. Four mugs with varying amounts of dark liquid rested on the desk. The surface of the desk was cluttered with stacks of paper and folders. Martinez was a slob.

The top drawer of a four-drawer putty-colored filing cabinet was open. Manila folders were crammed in willy-nilly. Other than the desk and filing cabinet, the room was bare except for a dusty, cheap Bentwood coat rack in a corner. It stood at a weird angle, like it was put together incorrectly. Nothing on the walls except stains, including blood and worse from Martinez's head.

I couldn't figure it out. I carefully stepped around the desk to get a look at Martinez's computer. On the screen was a spreadsheet program. I glanced at the details, but it was just a bunch of numbers to me.

There were two exit wounds in the back of Martinez's head. I checked the wall and looked around the floor for bullets and casings. Someone was a fucking pro because there weren't any.

I was tempted to poke around further, but decided it made more sense to get out. I went back into the hall and followed it to a different stairway. This one led me outside to an alley. From there, I made my way back to the parking lot.

Part of me was relieved. Every time I do something like this, I wonder if my fucking ass will get caught. Someone else could worry this time. For less than a second, I thought about pretending to Rosa that I'd done it. It would be a stupid lie, designed only to make me look better. I needed to grow the fuck up. I despise people who take credit for things other people do.

TWELVE

Rosa was typing on her laptop at the kitchen island when I walked in. She stopped, hands hanging in the air, and nodded, eager for me to get to the point.

"Someone got to him first," I said. "He was dead when I got there."

Her mouth dropped open. "You're joking, right?"

"Nope. Dude was shot." I pointed to two places on my forehead to show the wounds.

Rosa was on the verge of asking me if I was sure, but, fortunately, realized how stupid the question was. She glanced down at her computer and started typing again. I walked behind her and looked at the screen. She'd pulled up *The Miami Herald*.

"It's not reported yet," she said.

"That's not surprising," I said. "Anybody's guess when they discover the body."

"Bizarre." Rosa looked back at me. "Seems like a strange coincidence, doesn't it, Kell?"

"It does."

"Did you see anyone?"

"No."

"I don't even know what to say."

I shrugged. "You said he wasn't well liked. You were right. Have you heard from Valerie?"

She nodded. "She's still at the hospital. They're running tests. They think he's had another heart attack. He's conscious but groggy."

"Will she come back tonight?"

"She might stay with Aunt Marie."

I was disappointed to hear this, but I had no business having expectations. If Valerie didn't show up, it'd be Rosa and me, and we had a hard time keeping our hands off each other. It might be breaking some rule, but Rosa was Rosa. I wasn't much better.

"Could you tell how long he'd been dead?" Rosa asked.

"He wasn't there the first time and the blood, well, it had to be recent. Real recent. An hour or so at the most."

"You saw his car?"

"Yes."

"You're sure that maybe you didn't miss it the first time?"

Rosa was testing my patience. I gave her a look and willed myself not to get snotty.

"It's just odd," she said, apologizing.

We heard Valerie's car door slam in the driveway.

"They've admitted him for observation," she said, after she'd hurried in, face dented with worry. "They want to keep him overnight. With any luck, he can go home tomorrow. I took Aunt Marie home and will pick her up tomorrow morning."

Valerie glanced at me and waited. I didn't say anything.

"How'd it go?" she finally asked.

I kept quiet, expecting Rosa to fill her in.

"Something go wrong?" she asked, a note of panic in her voice.

"He was already dead," Rosa said.

Valerie tried to process the information but couldn't. "Already dead?" She repeated it like it was a foreign language.

"Someone got there before me," I said. "Just barely by the

looks of it."

"That doesn't make sense," she said. "Was he shot?"

I nodded. "We can't figure it out either."

Valerie looked at Rosa for an explanation. She had none.

"I guess it worked out for the best," Valerie said, still unsure.

"I guess," Rosa said. She was thinking, looking at all the angles, trying to cut through the puzzle. Good luck.

Valerie made another pizza for dinner, using the bread machine to make fresh dough. She then sautéed mushrooms and onions and tossed them on top with parmesan and shredded mozzarella.

"The trick," she said, when we were eating, "is to use semolina flour. Then bake it as high as your oven will go."

She was right because the pizza tasted like it came from a pizza place. It was tasty, but it bummed me out because it reminded me of Gretchen.

After dinner, I got an urge to call her. Rosa and Valerie were surfing the computer, trying to find out more about the murder. It had finally been reported, but the news was drib-drabbing in.

Gretchen told me not to call, but you know that feeling you get, and you can't control it? Well, I had it.

I went into my room, steeled myself, and called. It was eight o'clock in Miami, so it was five in California.

"Hey, Gretchen," I said, relieved that I didn't get her voice mail. "I'm sorry if I was short with you earlier. I wasn't trying to piss you off."

"I'm kind of busy right now," she said. She didn't say it like she was getting back at me. No, even worse, she said it like I'd caught her doing something. With someone.

"That's cool," I said. "I'm sorry. We'll talk later."

She hesitated like she wanted to say something. "Is it okay if I call later?"

I planned on having sex with Valerie and Rosa. I couldn't say that, could I?

"Sure," I said.

If I was getting busy, she'd have to leave a voice mail.

"It might not be until tomorrow," Gretchen said.

"No problem," I said, immediately jumping to the conclusion that she was spending the night with someone. Fucking fuck.

We hung up, and I meandered into the living room where Rosa and Valerie continued to study the computer screen. They barely noticed me.

I went outside and sank into a tan chaise lounge by the pool. Things felt off, unsettled. I was outside for a half hour when my phone rang.

"Sorry," Gretchen said. "I was at dinner. With Gin," she quickly added, like she wanted to ease my paranoia. Bless her.

"How's Thuggie?"

"He misses you."

"Aw." Good boy, I thought. "I miss him too."

It was true. When Gretchen taught class, he never let me out of his sight. Yeah, partly it was that he never knew when I'd get the urge to take him for a walk, but I think he genuinely loved me. We were buddies.

"You too," I said.

She didn't say anything.

"Awkward silence," I said.

"Yeah. Maybe it's too soon to talk."

"So we're back on the 'You don't want me to call' thing?"

"I need to clear my head, so I can make some decisions. Do I have any mail?"

"Nothing important."

"Would you do me a favor and read off the return labels?" Gretchen asked.

"I'm not home right now."

"Oh." The 'oh' sounded like she figured I was at a sleazy hotel with a tattooed blonde stripper.

"I'm at the park," I said.

"Isn't it late?"

"It's still light. I'm just walking."

"You alone?"

I winced. I shouldn't have told Gretchen I'd met Debra at the park.

"All by myself," I said. "Absolutely, totally alone."

"Thuggie would be jealous if he knew you were at the p-a-r-k." Gretchen spelled it because Thuggie has a fucking fit if you say the word in his presence. I suspected he was on Gretchen's lap.

"I'm alone," I said.

"Be careful," Gretchen said. "Remember, someone got killed there a few years ago."

Yeah, poor Hank Kingsley. It was me. I'd done the hit before I met Gretchen. It was still big news in the area.

"There's plenty of people around," I said. "I'm safe."

"Promise me you'll leave before it gets too dark."

"I promise. Is Gin okay?" I asked, wanting to change the subject.

"Yeah. She has a light teaching load, so we've been taking some daytrips."

"Larry been around?"

"Yeah." Gretchen wasn't a huge fan of Larry's. She'd never warmed up to him. "Too much."

"He's not that bad."

She didn't say anything. Sensing she was on the verge of getting off the phone, I beat her to it.

"I need to go," I said. "I'll leave it up to you on when we can talk again."

This time when we hung up, I was even more bummed. I didn't know the worst was yet to come.

THIRTEEN

I stared at the moon for a half hour or so, streaming morose thoughts about how I'd probably be alone the rest of my fucking life and how sad it was. "Along Again (Naturally)" dropped in my head, and I wondered if anyone had committed suicide because they couldn't get a fucking song out of their fucking head.

While pondering this, a commotion came from inside the house. Rosa's voice was raised but undecipherable. Then my name was called.

"Kell!"

Rosa's voice had almost the same tone and cadence as my mom's shout when I was in trouble. In fact, the sound took me right back to my childhood, just like Proust's madeleine cookie. No, I haven't read Proust, but Gretchen told me about it. Before I had a chance to say, 'Huh,' the sliding glass door screeched open, and Rosa and Valerie hurtled outside.

"What have you done?" Rosa asked, armed outstretched. "What the *fuck* have you done?" She stumbled toward me, her right hand in a fist.

I scrambled out of the chaise.

"What did you do?" Rosa pleaded.

I wondered if she was mad because I'd called Gretchen, but that didn't make sense.

"Why? Oh my God, Kell." Rosa's face was a contorted mess of hurt, anger, and shock. She's given me lots of looks in the time

I've known her. I've never seen this one. It scared the hell out of me.

"What happened?" I asked. I looked at Valerie. Her expression was similar to Rosa's.

"Did you fucking set me up?" Rosa asked.

I shook my head.

"Tell me," Rosa said. "What did you do?"

"When?" I asked.

My baffled look infuriated her.

Valerie mumbled something that sounded like, "She's getting arrested."

"*What?* Rosa, I have no idea what's going on. Tell me what happened."

"Do you have any idea why I'm the chief suspect in the Martinez murder?" Rosa asked.

"*You?*" I asked.

"Me," Rosa said. "I have to meet with my lawyer tomorrow for questioning. He said there's a chance I'll be arrested." She was breathing hard. Her words were like thrown pellets.

Rosa and I have been through a lot together. I've never seen her have a complete, total meltdown. She's usually cool, but she was losing it big-time.

"What did you do?" she asked. "What the fuck, Kell? Why? What are you thinking? You think you'll get my business? Get my girl?"

'Get my business? Get my girl?' It was dialogue from a bad movie.

"I didn't do anything," I said.

Rosa went on and on, mostly saying the same things. Then she started crying. She wiped her face with her hands and forearms and stalked back inside, followed closely by Valerie.

I stayed outside for a few minutes. Frankly, I was afraid to go inside. I finally got up my courage to walk in, wondering if I'd get jumped.

No one attacked me, but I found Rosa sitting white-faced on the couch with a mound of tissues on her lap. Valerie stood over her.

Rosa looked up at me. "Just tell me," she said softly. "You win, but tell me how you did it. You left something incriminating the second time you went," she said, thinking. "You said he wasn't there the first time, but that's when you killed him. It didn't make sense that he wasn't there. What did you leave behind? My fingerprints? A personal belonging?" Rosa stood, glancing around. "Did you take something from here?" She sat back down. "What did you do the second time? Anything? Did you decide to do it because I sent you out twice? That doesn't make sense. Why come back here? I don't get it, Kell."

"He wasn't there the first time," I said. "The second time he was already dead. I didn't do anything to implicate you. I swear to you. Why would I do that?"

Rosa acted like she didn't hear me. "I don't understand why you'd do this. I thought we worked through everything." She shook her head and lowered her eyes. "I never saw it coming. I never thought you'd do me like this. I trusted you, Kell. I can't even protect myself because I don't know what you've done. Did someone pay you to do it? Who?" Her mind worked like a computer, analyzing dozens of if-then statements.

"Rosa, listen to me." I tried to get her to look me in the eye. "I haven't done anything. I haven't set you up. I don't know what's going on."

"My God," Rosa said, "my parents will be so ashamed." She cried again. Valerie comforted her, murmuring inaudible words.

I stood there like a big dummy. "I swear, Rosa. I swear to God. On my parents' graves." That got her attention. I only said this when I really meant something. My parents were killed in a car accident when I was sixteen. Rosa had been their babysitter and an employee in their art gallery. She liked them and vice versa. After their death, I eventually ended up living with her, and one thing led to another. Anyway, when I say anything about their fucking graves, well, it's super serious.

"Then you obviously fucked up somehow," Rosa said, wiping her face. "Always hire a professional. You were out of practice. You fucked up."

"Maybe I did," I said, "but I don't see how." The insults stung.

"They must have evidence tying me to his murder," Rosa said. "I'll probably be arrested." She sobbed again. "I can't fight if I don't know what you did."

"I don't get it," I said. I didn't. I kept running things through my head. How could anything implicate Rosa? Unless they had emails or something like that, but Rosa was too smart to leave a trail. "If someone framed you, it wasn't me."

I looked at Valerie. I had a bad feeling that she might be behind the scheme but couldn't wrap my head around it. All I knew was that I hadn't done it.

Rosa stared at me, trying to figure out if I was lying. I kneeled at her feet and took her damp hands. "I'll get you out of this," I said. "I promise."

Valerie didn't want me touching Rosa. She made a move toward me. I stood and stepped away.

"I'll fix it," I said. "I don't know how, but I will."

"You honestly haven't set me up?" Rosa asked.

"I would never set you up. Never. You don't know anything about the evidence they supposedly have?"

"I need to meet with my attorney," she said. She took a deep breath, glanced at a clock, and winced. "God, what will I tell my parents?"

Rosa's parents were a big deal in the small town where we grew up. Her father was a surgeon, and her mother was the hospital's dietician. They'd retired a year or so ago and moved to Arizona. They had no idea what Rosa had done in the past. This would throw them for sure.

"Tell me the truth," Rosa said. "Kell, if you did it, tell me. I need to know what I'm dealing with."

"I didn't do it," I said. "I'm more shocked than you are."

"You can't possibly be more shocked than I am."

It was almost a light moment, but no one smiled.

"I can't think of any reason why you're a suspect," I said. "None. How did you find out?"

"Ray called me," she said. "He got a heads up from someone in the police department. They want to question me tomorrow. They told him I'd probably be booked. They wanted to come tonight, but he promised them I'd show. It doesn't make sense. How could I be a suspect?"

It wasn't easy to think with the looks I was getting from Rosa and Valerie.

"Have you confided in anyone?" Rosa asked me.

"Absolutely not. Who would I tell?" I looked at Valerie. "What about you? Did you confide in anyone?"

Valerie shot me a nasty look. Rosa made a disgusted noise.

"No. I haven't fucking *confided* in anyone," Valerie said in my face.

I resisted the strong temptation to shove her. "How else could anyone know?" I asked Rosa. "Someone had to say something to someone."

"Kell," Rosa said, "Valerie didn't tell anyone. It's ridiculous. I certainly didn't say anything either. Only the three of us know the plan."

"I'm not the weak link," I said. "I haven't said anything. You and I have never had a phone call about it." I looked again at Valerie.

"You are fucking unreal," Valerie said.

I thought she might come at me, but Rosa took her arm. "Let it go, Valerie," she said. "Come on. Let's go back and get a plan for tomorrow."

They walked to their bedroom and left me. I kept thinking

someone would return and tell me something, even to get the hell out, but no one did. I went to my room and sat on the bed, thinking.

I occasionally heard Rosa and Valerie talking in low voices. I wondered if they were plotting against me. I was getting all conspiracy-minded. If someone wanted to set us against each other, they'd done an excellent job.

FOURTEEN

Unable to sleep, I got out of bed a little after two and crept quietly and carefully into the living room, slumped onto the sofa, and picked up Rosa's iPad. I pulled up *The Miami Herald* and read about the murder. Rosa wasn't mentioned, but the article said the police had several strong leads.

"What are you doing?"

Rosa, dressed in a dark, monk-like robe, stood in the hallway.

"I'm reading stories from the newspaper, trying to figure it out," I said.

I couldn't see her well because of the darkness, but what I saw frightened me. Rosa looked old. She'd aged ten years that night. She stood bent at an angle, hugging the robe closed. She was a pathetic sight, and I couldn't take it. I looked down at the screen.

"What'd you figure out?" she asked. There was no inflection in her voice. I couldn't read her.

"Nothing. There's not enough here to see what they have. Rosa, there's nothing they could have."

"Do you have your gun?"

I was afraid I knew why she was asking. It had already occurred to me that Rosa would never go to prison.

"Kell?"

"Yeah," I said.

She didn't say anything.

"Why?" I asked.

"I was wondering if you left it at his office. With my fingerprints. I'm sure you could figure out how to do something like that."

Momentarily relieved that she didn't want to kill herself, I was upset that she was still thought I'd framed her.

"I never pulled out the gun," I said. "There was no need to. I didn't frame you, Rosa."

"Was it because of the Atlanta thing? I wish you'd just killed me. This is far worse, but you knew that, didn't you?"

"If I was ever going to kill you, it would have been after I came back from Atlanta. I didn't. This isn't me. I don't care what it looks like. It isn't me. You know Valerie better than me, but maybe she—"

"It's not Valerie. It's over, isn't it?" Rosa asked. "It's all over."

"No," I said. "All you have to do is tell the police the truth. About where you were and when. The truth is on your side." I sounded like an idiot.

Rosa sighed loudly and shook her head. "Go to bed, Kell."

"What's she doing?" It was Valerie's voice.

"Nothing," Rosa said.

"Come on, honey," Valerie coaxed. "You need to sleep."

Rosa numbly turned and shuffled off in Valerie's direction. I refreshed the screen. There were no new updates.

I went back to my room and sat on the bed, going over all the steps I'd taken. Nothing led to Rosa's arrest. I thought about telling Rosa I was delayed by Gretchen's phone call but decided against it. It made me look bad, unprofessional.

I came out of my room the next morning when I heard Rosa

and Valerie murmuring, closing doors. Rosa had pulled herself together and looked like a million bucks, a socialite on her way to a business meeting. She'd showered, dressed, put on makeup, and wore a classy red dress.

She barely glanced at me. I was invisible. They left without saying a word to me.

I went on the laptop and read the updated stories. Again, there was nothing about Rosa. I learned that Martinez was divorced three times and had three kids. The newspaper described him as a "real estate investor."

Hours later, Valerie returned home. She did her best to avoid me, sweeping past me and heading for the bedroom.

"Valerie," I called after her.

She reluctantly turned when her hand reached the doorknob.

"What happened?" I asked.

"She's being questioned by the police," she said. "The problem is that I was at the hospital, so she doesn't have an alibi."

"She could use me."

"We've decided not to involve you. It's best that no one knows about you. That you're here. That you came here."

I nodded. It bothered me that they were making decisions without my input. It bothered me more that they wanted to erase my presence in Miami.

"Can she come back to the house today?" I asked.

Valerie shrugged. "We don't know."

"Is there anything I can do?"

Valerie shook her head. "She thinks it's you."

"She said that?"

Valerie nodded. "I do too."

"I think it's you." I'd been going over things in my head. Whatever evidence the police had could have been provided by Valerie. Other than me, there was no one Rosa trusted as much.

How trustworthy was Valerie? She'd betrayed me in Atlanta. Maybe she did the same to Rosa in Miami.

Valerie shook her head. "I would never do anything like that." She released the door knob and took a step toward me.

"Me either," I said.

"It looks like you did something."

"I could make an argument it was you. You were the only other person who knew what her plans were. You could have done something."

"How?" she asked.

"Not sure, but you could have framed her."

"Why would I? We've got a great thing going. Business is great. Our relationship is great. I have no motive."

"Money," I said.

She looked at me like I was crazy. "If Rosa's not in the picture, there is no money. It wouldn't make sense for me to mess things up. She *is* the company. I can't do it on my own."

"Maybe you're angry at her."

"Why would I be angry?"

"You tell me. Maybe because she brought me here."

Valerie slapped me. It was a good one too. It stung my cheek and turned my head. I tested my jaw. Her hand was in a fist. She wanted to hit me again.

"You're no threat to me," she said in a choked voice.

I'm not the voice of reason, patience, or restraint in most situations. I struggled to keep my temper. "That's not what I meant," I said. "I swear to you I didn't do anything to hurt Rosa."

"Neither did I. One of us is lying."

"It's not me."

I took a step forward. She took a step back and raised her fists.

"Let's say neither of us is lying," I said. "You seem sincere. I know I didn't do it. There's someone out there who's at least a step ahead of us. We need to quit this." I motioned from her to me. "And figure out who the fuck is responsible."

"Everything points to you."

"If I'd done it, do you think I would have stayed in Miami? The smart thing would have been to get the fuck out. Not come back here like a big dummy."

"Unless you didn't want it to look like you did it. Maybe you wanted to revel in it."

"Do I seem like that? Work with me on this, Valerie."

"I don't trust you," she said, and headed to the bedroom door again.

"Valerie."

She stopped.

"We need to work together," I said, resisting the temptation to grab hold of her.

She turned.

"I'm on your side," I said.

She narrowed her eyes and took a step forward. "What the fuck does that mean?"

I could see how she might misinterpret this. "I'm on your side and Rosa's side."

"Maybe you should go," she said. "Go back to Georgia. I need to deal with Rosa. And Uncle Buddy."

Uncle Buddy. I'd forgotten about him. "How's he doing?" I asked.

"Don't feign concern."

Something in my expression made her lower her eyes. "He's been released," she said. "I took him home to Aunt Marie."

She'd had a busy morning.

"Does he know about Rosa?" I asked. This would obviously be a huge blow to him. Maybe they'd try to keep it from him.

"Ray talked to him," she said. "He's pulling some strings. Calling in favors. That kind of thing. Who knows?"

With that, she went inside her bedroom. The door clicked

shut, and the lock slid into place.

I clenched my teeth. First of all, I respect a fucking closed door. Second, it's a flimsy door. I could kick the fucking thing down with one kick, lock or no lock. Part of me wanted to continue the discussion with Valerie. Another part wondered if I was a damn fool for arguing with her.

I walked to my room and locked the door. Hell, for all I knew Rosa had instructed Valerie to return to the house and shoot me. It wasn't a great plan, but none of us were clicking on all cylinders.

I dialed Larry. He answered on the fourth ring which was a good thing because I didn't want to leave a message. I was unraveling.

"Yeah?" he said.

"I'm in a jam, Larry."

"You're what?"

"In a jam."

"I thought you said in a jail."

He laughed. I didn't.

"Where are you?" he asked.

"Miami."

"What kind of jam?"

"All hell's broken loose," I said. "Rosa is a suspect for a hit she didn't do. She thinks I set her up."

"Want me to come?"

I was touched. "Would you?"

"Absolutely. I'll tell Gin something and get the next flight out." Guess he figured he owed me since he'd helped screw up things with Gretchen. Sort of.

Larry called back a few minutes later with his flight information. I wasn't sure what he could do, but he knew lots of people, and I'd seen him work magic. Plus, I wanted moral support. I wasn't the most popular person in Miami right now.

Before I left, I knocked on Valerie's door.

"Yeah," she called out after a few seconds.

"Valerie, I'm going out for a while."

"Okay."

"I don't know when I'll be back."

"Okay."

"But I am coming back."

"All right."

I couldn't get a gauge on her voice. She was distracted, like when you're on the telephone with someone.

"I'm leaving right now," I said.

"Okay."

"I'll be back sometime today."

"Fine."

FIFTEEN

I drove around, killing time, until it got close to when Larry's flight arrived. I hate airports because I hate waiting around for someone or something. I parked at Miami International Airport, went inside, bought a *Wired*, sat and, yes, waited. Larry's flight was delayed, but finally it showed up.

I hugged him when he got off the plane. I'm not a hugger, so it surprised him.

"I'm scared," I said, close to his ear.

He thought I was putting him on, so he pulled me back to look at my face.

Concern washed across his features. "It'll be okay," he told me. I wanted to believe him.

Larry was hungry, so we ended up at the Eleventh Street Diner on Washington. Larry ordered a Monte Cristo and a Coke. I wasn't hungry but figured I needed to eat something. I ordered a cheese omelet and a cup of coffee.

"How's Gretchen?" I asked.

"She's okay. To be honest, it was a relief to get out of there. It's like an Oprah marathon every day. Hormonal City."

"Does she talk about me?"

He nodded. "She and Gin talk about you a lot. Over and over. You know how women are. Tell me what's going on with Rosa."

I leaned forward and lowered my voice. "Larry, help me figure this out. Maybe I'm not seeing the obvious here."

I glanced around. The restaurant was filled with young couples who were more interested in their dramas than mine. Still, I'm paranoid by nature. Larry leaned in so I could whisper.

"Rosa asked me to take care of a guy," I said. He blinked and moved his jaw back and forth. "She told me he was there all the time. I went, but he wasn't there. I came back to her house. After a few hours, she sent me again. He was there, but someone had already taken care of him. That night, Rosa finds out she's the chief suspect. She might be arrested by now. She thinks I framed her. So does her girlfriend Valerie."

He was quiet for a long time. "I don't get it," he finally said.

"I don't either."

"Could it be Valerie? If she's accusing you—"

"I guess she's got motive, but it's not really her thing."

He was thinking. "Someone double-crossed Rosa," he said, gulping down his Coke. "What do you think, Kell?"

I threw up my hands. "I can't grasp it. I could understand someone framing me. That'd be easy. But Rosa? If there were witnesses who saw something, well, we don't look anything alike. Why say it was Rosa? And how did they know she was planning something? That's why I keep going back to Valerie. Rosa wouldn't have told anyone else. I start thinking maybe someone bugged the house. I've even thought maybe someone was in the house, you know, hidden, listening to us."

He processed what I said. "Who would do that?"

"I don't know. They have tons of people come through. You know, house cleaners, renovators, the marble guy, the pool dude, the tile dyke."

"They have a marble guy?"

"Yeah, and he seems to have a thing for Valerie."

"Does she have a thing for him?"

I shook my head. "No."

He thought about it and shook his head. "I don't think so, Kell. What's a tile dyke?"

"Risa Rispoli. I don't think it's her. She cleans and repairs the tile." Since we'd hit it off, I wanted to protect her. "I'd be shocked if it turns out she had something to do with it. But who knows. Like I said, there were lots of people coming in and out of the house."

"Who would have a motive?"

"I don't know. I thought about the intern too. Dana. Valerie described her as ambitious. She is."

Larry made a face. "A student intern?"

"Maybe she's got a crush on Valerie and wants to get Rosa out of the way."

Larry played with his napkin. "You know for sure she's got a crush on Valerie?"

I thought about telling him that I was damn sure she had a crush on me. Instead, I shrugged.

"How old is she?" he asked.

"I don't know. Early twenties, I guess."

He shook his head. "You're thinking it's *All About Eve*?"

I nodded. Sometimes when Larry and I work something, we're holed up in a hotel room and end up watching old movies. I've seen *All About Eve* a few times.

"Understudy sabotaging the lead? I don't see it, Kell."

I leaned in. "See, Larry, there's something else. I know what you'll say, so hear me out."

"Tell me." He motioned me to hurry the fuck up.

"I didn't tell Rosa this." Larry shot me his impatient look. "I was delayed in getting to the dude's office the second time. Slightly."

He took several large bites of his sandwich. I took a couple quick bites of my omelet.

"I got a call from Gretchen as I was walking toward the building," I said.

"You had your phone on?"

"I took the call. I know. Not like me at all. But I did. I hadn't heard from her in weeks. I couldn't miss her call."

"How long did you talk?"

"Just a few minutes. By the time I got there—"

Larry nodded. "Let's go back to your car and talk some more."

I paid the bill, and we hustled back to the Mustang.

The walk from the restaurant to my car was miserable. We were sweating buckets by the time we got inside. Who could get used to this? I turned on the engine and cranked the air.

"You know what I'm thinking, don't you?" he asked, adjusting the vents nearest him to blow in his face.

"I walked into a setup."

"It's too much of a coincidence that Martinez was killed minutes before you got there," he said. "If you hadn't stopped to talk to Gretchen, you'd have run into the killer. Colliding hit men? It seems like a setup to me, Kell. My guess is that whoever killed Martinez was supposed to kill you. Maybe make it look like a murder-suicide. Whoever it was got spooked and left before you showed up. Who'd set you up?"

I knew what he was getting at. "When I came back, Rosa didn't look the least bit surprised to see me turn up alive. I would have seen something in her face. I think." I thought for a moment. "Maybe Rosa could have put on a nice act. I don't think Valerie could. It's too bad Valerie wasn't there."

"Where was she?"

"She was called out of the house after I came back the first time because Uncle Buddy was taken to the hospital."

"Do you think it was arranged on purpose that Valerie wasn't there?"

"I'm fairly sure she was at the hospital," I said. "We could check to make sure Uncle Buddy was admitted, but he's elderly and has health issues. When Valerie returned, she wasn't surprised to see me."

"Maybe Rosa contacted her when you were gone. Maybe Valerie didn't know you were supposed to walk into something bad. I hate to tell you this, Kell, but if I had to make a guess I'd say that Rosa was planning a twofer. That's what it looks like. You need to think about the possibility. I don't know the girl. You do. But on the face of it, that's what it looks like."

The thought had crossed my mind. It'd have to since she'd tried to kill me once before.

"Why would she kill me?" I finally asked. "I'm useful to her. We get along. Really well. She practically begged me to come to Miami."

"I don't claim to understand women, Kell. It's just a theory. Who else knew you were in Miami?"

"A bunch of people saw me. It's not like she hid me. All the people that came to the house. She took me into the office a few times. Dolores, Dana, Uncle Buddy, Aunt Marie. If it came out I'd been killed with Martinez, and they had my picture, I think someone would have said, 'Hey, wasn't that the chick who was staying with Rosa?'"

"People don't read newspapers anymore."

"It'd be on TV then. Maybe I'm a sap, but I can't see it. It also doesn't explain how Rosa ended up getting framed. It's more complicated."

He nodded. "You're right. It doesn't explain the frame. Valerie?"

"She's not dumb, but she's no Rosa. I mean, Rosa's a genius at figuring out stuff. I can't see Valerie coming up with something like this. She's crazy about Rosa."

"Can you think of anyone else who could have possibly had knowledge of any of this?"

"The only other thing I can come up with is that it's someone like the marble guy," I said.

"Or tile dyke."

"Someone who overheard us. Maybe Dana. Someone who wanted something Rosa had. Or hated her."

"I doubt you were planning this with a houseful of people listening in."

"That's the thing. We generally talked about it late at night. Maybe Rosa and Valerie said something when I wasn't around. Or maybe they said something in their building, but I don't see them doing that. Rosa's too careful. She's your caliber, Larry."

He liked that and puffed out his chest a bit.

"Maybe we can look around the house and see if someone could have gotten in and heard something," I said. "I don't think there's a basement, but maybe there's a crawl space."

Larry shook his head. "I don't see it, Kell. The marble guy? Hate Rosa enough to frame her? That's a lot of trouble when all he has to do is pry loose some expensive marble. Or scratch it with a car key. Unless he has some connection with the dead guy, but that's a stretch."

I sat back and blew air out my mouth.

Larry was gentle with me. "You've got blinders on. I don't. Let me talk to Valerie. If Rosa's got a good lawyer, she's probably already back home."

"You think so?"

"You do know that the rich are treated different in the criminal justice system? Shocking, isn't it?"

He got a brief smile from me.

"I don't know what they've got on her," I said, "but I can't let her go to prison. If we don't figure it out, Larry, I'm thinking—"

He looked at me like I was crazy. "Whoa."

"She couldn't stand to be in prison. I could take it better."

"Slow down. Why are you so stupid over this girl? Good God, Kell. Go to prison for her?" Larry made a face.

"I don't care," I said, my voice breaking. "I really don't." Bam. Just like that, I bawled like a four-year-old. Next thing I knew, Larry had his big old arms around me, consoling me. A few pedestrians looked into the car and quickly looked away. They thought the big lug had broken up with me, busted up my heart good.

Larry let me cry for a good while. Then he cleared his throat.

"You're depressed because of Gretchen," he said. "You're not thinking straight. Hey, I'm not trying to give you false hope or anything, but it's possible Gretchen is having second thoughts."

I pulled away and scrutinized him.

"Like I said, I don't know anything," Larry said. "She's been crying a lot."

Crying? Sounded like a good sign to me.

"A lot," he said, shuddering.

"She said she was seeing someone."

"I don't think that's working out."

"Maybe she's crying over her."

"Maybe."

This deflated me.

"But I think it's you," he said. "No one tells me anything, but I get the feeling she misses you."

This was the best news I'd heard in a while.

"Is Gin sticking up for me?" I asked.

He moved his hand back and forth. "Yes and no. She wants Gretchen to be happy. She's not sure you can do that."

"Does she want me to be happy?"

"The whole lying and cheating thing—"

I needed to pull myself together. I wiped my face with the back of my hand.

"We'll get through this, Kell," Larry said. He struggled to pull his handkerchief from his jeans pocket and then handed it to me. "You want to go to prison because your heart's broken. That's crazy. You'll feel different in a day or two. Let me talk to Valerie and hopefully Rosa too. We can figure this out. Does Rosa own a gun?"

I blew my nose and wiped my face. "I don't know. I don't think so. She hates guns."

He gave me a look.

"They make her nervous."

"Does Valerie have a gun?"

"I doubt it. Why?"

"I don't know what we're walking into."

I laughed. "You big scaredy-cat. You think they'll shoot us?"

"If they don't know what our intentions are, they might. You've got your gun?"

"Of course." It would have been stupid to leave it at Rosa's. "Do you have one?"

"Unfortunately, no," he said.

"Larry, it's two girly girls. Valerie can't shoot. I've never seen Rosa handle a gun."

Larry wasn't convinced.

"Rosa's got enough trouble," I said.

"Did you see her get the phone call from the lawyer?"

I shook my head. "I was outside. She came out and told me about it."

"There's always the possibility," he said, "that she lied. That she never got a phone call saying she was a suspect. That when she left this morning she didn't go to the police."

"Then look out Jennifer Lawrence, Rosa Gold is getting the Oscar this year. She had a complete meltdown last night. Went totally crazy."

"I'm just saying."

I tried to pass the handkerchief back to Larry, but he recoiled like I was handing him actual boogers. I stuffed it in my own pocket.

"I'll walk in first, and then you can come in if I don't get killed," I said, starting the car engine.

SIXTEEN

I was twitchy by the time we pulled up to Rosa's house. Valerie's SUV was parked in a different place than when I left. The Jag was still in the garage.

Larry's eye moved around like he was prey. "Don't you think we should knock first?"

"You big chicken," I taunted, when we walked up the sidewalk.

"I'm cautious. Would it kill you to—?"

"Quit being a fucking baby. Like I said, I'll go in first."

"They might not appreciate you—"

I punched in the security code and tried the door. No dice. I tried again. Same result. "Goddamn it. They changed the fucking code." I rapped hard on the solid wood door. "Valerie, it's me. Open the fucking door."

"Maybe she's not home," Larry said.

"She's here. I'll knock the fucking window out." I pretended to look around for an object to toss through the window. My temper still surprises Larry, but I know how far I can go.

"Hold on, Kell." Larry knocked hard with a closed fist. "Sheriff's department, ma'am," he said in a booming voice. "Open the door."

Larry looked like he might be with the sheriff's department. He has a law enforcement look to begin with, and today he wore a navy windbreaker and blue jeans.

Larry got results. Valerie opened the door.

"What the fuck?" I said, pushing past her. I pointed back at Larry. "This is Larry. He's here to help."

I strolled into the kitchen to get a soft drink, but stopped in my tracks. Rosa was leaning against the kitchen counter. Dressed in the same outfit she'd left in, she was drained, frail.

"Did they let you go?" I asked.

She had a strange expression on her face. It took me a moment to realize it was fear. She was afraid of me.

"This is my brother-in-law," I said, when Larry caught up to me. "I've filled him in on the deets. He's cool."

"I'm Larry Howell," he said, and held his hand out toward Rosa. She took a step forward and shook it. I wondered if this was something I would come to regret. They scanned each other like crazy.

"I've heard a lot about you," Larry said. "It's a pleasure to finally meet you."

"Thank you," Rosa said. "Same here. Kell, could I have a moment with you, please?"

I grabbed a Dr. Pepper from the fridge, and Rosa led me off to the living room. Valerie asked Larry if he wanted something to drink. I didn't hear his reply. Rosa took hold of the front of my shirt. It wasn't a violent move, more of a clutching, needy thing. She was inches from my face.

"Kell, on a scale from zero to one hundred, how much do you trust this guy?" she asked.

"One hundred."

She stared at me a long time. "God, I hope you're right," she said, releasing my shirt.

"Did they decide not to charge you?" I asked, when Rosa and I walked back to the kitchen. I said it loud enough for Larry to hear.

"So far," she said. "But they could come for me any minute." She spoke tentatively, still unsure what she should say in front of Larry.

"What did you tell your parents?" I asked.

"That none of it was true."

"How'd they take it?" I asked.

She lowered her head. "They believe me. They offered money for lawyers. They think someone's jealous of my success." Rosa was embarrassed because she'd been pulling the wool over their eyes for a long time. They thought she was a successful businesswoman who'd done things by the book. The thought of disappointing her parents bothered her more than prison, and, believe me, Rosa didn't want to go to prison.

She also didn't want her name muddied in the press. She hates scandal. This was juicy, and Miami was abuzz.

"They want to come here," Rosa said. "To support me. I hope I've talked them out of it."

"Larry's got some ideas." I didn't know if he did, but I wanted to encourage Rosa.

"Kell's filled me in on a lot," Larry said. "I assume you haven't been charged?"

"No," Rosa said.

"One thing I recommend right away," he said, "is you get a criminal defense attorney. I understand you're using the company attorney. I know a really good—"

"I'm happy with the representation I have," Rosa said in a guarded, business-like tone.

"With all due respect," Larry said, "I assume your present attorney specializes in business, maybe real estate transactions. You need a criminal attorney for something like this." His tone was polite and gentle.

"I'm happy that I haven't been arrested," she said. "I'm loyal. I'll stick with Ray. Uncle Buddy vouched for him, told me the guy is first-rate."

"I admire your loyalty," he said. "But you need to hire the best person for the job. You don't have to make the decision right now, but think about it. I strongly recommend you contact Sylvia Wright. She's here in Miami. She's a take-no-prisoners criminal defense attorney. I've seen her make grown men cry. For one thing, she never would have let you be questioned."

"They made it seem like I'd be arrested if I didn't answer questions," Rosa said.

"It doesn't work like that," he said.

"I'll think about it." She was indeed thinking. In fact, she probably thought what I was thinking. She'd made a rookie mistake and wondered if it'd come back to haunt her.

Larry looked around. "Is there a place where we can sit and talk?" he asked.

Rosa motioned him to the oval glass table near the sliding glass door. He pulled out one of the black and chrome chairs and motioned for us to sit. We sat. Larry pulled out a notebook and pen from the satchel he'd carried inside.

"What kinds of questions did the police ask you?" he asked Rosa.

"Mostly whereabouts," she said.

"For the time of the murder?" he asked.

"Yes."

"What else?" he asked.

"Feelings I had about Martinez," she said. "Any negativity we've had in the past."

"Did you have any?"

"Not publically. I said no."

"What else?"

Rosa shrugged. "That was mainly it. Most of it was about where I was Saturday afternoon."

"That's good news," Larry said.

Rosa tilted her head. "Why's that? I'm sorry. I'm usually more clear-headed. I didn't get much sleep last night." She was moving her body, acting girly.

"Understandable," he said in his most masculine voice. "I was afraid they were going after you for conspiracy. That'd be a lot more complicated. They think you were the trigger person."

"Someone ID'd me," Rosa said.

"That's what I'm thinking," he said. "Look, we've got to get some things out of the way. You suspect Kell."

I was content to remain quiet. For one thing, I liked watching the interaction between Larry and Rosa.

Rosa glanced at me, started to say something, and then stopped. "We have a history," she finally said. "She may have a motive."

"Kell told me she didn't have anything to do with it. If she said she didn't have anything to do with it, she didn't." He looked hard at Rosa. "She doesn't lie. I'd trust her with my life. I *have* trusted her with my life."

Larry laid it on a thick. I raised my eyebrows to let him know he could cool it.

"I agree with you," Rosa said. "I've known her since she was little. She's loyal. I certainly don't want to suspect her."

"I haven't known her that long, but long enough," Larry said.

"I trust her," Rosa said. "I just don't understand who could possibly implicate me. You're right, though. That's why I was upset at her betrayal."

They were trying to out-Kell each other. It was fascinating but weird. In truth, I was loyal, but I've always been a horrible liar. I've lied to everyone in the room tons of times.

"Okay, she's loyal and trustworthy," Valerie snapped. "Let's try to figure out what happened."

"Now that I've established that Kell is honest as the day is long," Larry said, "I have to tell you something. She kept something from you."

Rosa looked stricken. It hurt me to my core.

"What?" Valerie asked.

Rosa closed her eyes.

"It's not that bad," I said.

"Just tell me," Rosa said. She made two fists and put them on the table.

"When I went to Martinez's the second time," I said, "I parked in the lot you recommended. I walked to his building but stopped to take a phone call."

"You answered your phone?" Rosa was puzzled.

"Yeah. My phone rang."

"You had your phone on?" she asked.

"Yes."

"Good God, Kell," Rosa said.

"I'm totally out of practice with this thing," I said defensively. "It was Gretchen. I took the phone call. We talked for a while."

"So what?" Valerie asked. "Why is this important?" She wanted to say, 'Who the fuck cares?'

"It delayed me," I said.

Valerie looked at Rosa. Rosa looked at Larry and then got it.

"You think if she hadn't been delayed, she would have run into the hit man," Rosa said.

"That's right," Larry said.

Valerie still didn't get it.

"You think," Rosa said to Larry, but mostly for Valerie's benefit, "I set her up."

"We're getting everything out in the open, Rosa," I said. "Just say you didn't do it, and we can move on."

"Why didn't you tell me?" she asked me.

"I didn't want to look like a doofus," I said.

"So all this time you've been thinking I sent you off to be killed?" Rosa asked.

"Actually, it didn't occur to me until Larry pointed it out," I said. That wasn't entirely true, but I didn't want her to think I automatically suspected her.

"What would have happened if Kell and the other hit man got there at the same time?" Valerie asked. She was out of her league in this meeting.

"Hilarity would not ensue," I said.

"Who knew you went back out?" Rosa asked. She pointed to Larry's legal pad. "This is important. I think. Maybe someone was watching the house."

"Valerie knew," I said. "Right?"

"No," Valerie said.

"Yes, you did," Rosa said to Valerie. "I told you—"

"When you came back in," I said, "you looked at me and wanted to know what happened. You must have known I'd gone back out."

"She did," Rosa said. "I told her when she called from the hospital."

"That's right," Valerie said. "You did. I was upset because there'd been a delay on one of his tests. You said something like 'Kell went back out.'"

"But it was a half hour, maybe forty-five minutes after you left," Rosa said to Valerie. "Did you notice anyone watching when you left here?" she asked me.

I shook my head. "No," I said. "Something else I want to be clear about. Larry, if you don't mind, could I talk to Rosa privately for a minute?"

"Sure," he said.

"You want me to go too?" Valerie asked.

"I'd prefer it," I said.

Valerie wasn't happy about it, but she and Larry walked out to the patio and closed the sliding glass door. What I needed to talk to Rosa about was too personal to say in front of Larry, and I wasn't sure Rosa would be totally honest if Valerie was sitting next to us. I needed Rosa to look me in the eye when I asked.

"When you asked me to come here, you already knew you'd get me to kill Martinez, didn't you?" I asked in a rush.

She took her time to answer. "I honestly don't remember," Rosa said.

Gin, my psychology professor sister, once told me that whenever someone uses the word honestly in a sentence they're probably lying.

"Rosa, you and Valerie had sex with me to soften me up. You knew it'd be easy to get me to agree." I tried to keep anger out of my voice.

"We wanted to have sex with you," Rosa said.

"But you knew me. You knew it'd soften me."

"You could have said no."

"Did you have a plan B if I said no?"

"Plan B?"

"Would you get someone else to do it?"

"We never thought it through that far."

"Because you knew you could talk me into it."

"I wanted someone I could trust," Rosa said, "someone who wouldn't bungle it. It's not like I would have thrown you out if you didn't take the job. If you'd said no, it would have been cool."

"Before you asked me to come to Miami, you discussed it with Valerie."

"Of course I did. I wouldn't invite you without asking her."

"I mean, you discussed me taking out Martinez."

We stared at each other.

"I don't remember," she said.

"You might have?"

"It might have crossed my mind."

"And you talked about getting me all softened up so—"

"No." Rosa pointed her finger at me. "That's now how it went down. You're a hit man. A good one. We needed a good hit man. You're also someone I care about, who I like having sex with." She held up two fingers. "It's two separate things."

I closed my eyes. "It is so easy for you to work me," I said.

106

She reached across the table and grabbed my hand. "I swear to you I didn't set you up. If you'd said no, I wouldn't have been angry. We probably wouldn't have done anything. Just let it go. There was no plan B. We both should have realized it wasn't a good idea. I short-handed it. I didn't have much of a plan. Not like in the old days. And you." She made a face. "You had your phone on and took a call. No offense. But neither of us is good at this anymore."

She was right. She'd asked me, a washed-up hit man, to do the job. I half-assed the whole thing. We were lucky we weren't dead.

SEVENTEEN

I motioned Larry and Valerie back inside. They were finishing a conversation about the correct way to cook plantains. Valerie was more at ease. Larry has a way of doing that.

When we were all seated, everyone became quiet. Larry pulled out his legal pad and pen and read over his notes.

"All right," he said. "The last thing we talked about was Kell getting sent back. Rosa called Valerie about thirty to forty-five minutes—"

"No. I called her," Valerie said. "That's when she told me Kell had gone back."

Larry looked at me. "From the time you left here, how much time passed before you got to the office?" he asked.

Surprisingly, I wasn't that concerned with time. Normally, I would have been. "It took me maybe twenty minutes to get there," I said. "I drove on the street and saw his car. It took me maybe another five minutes to park my car in the lot and walk toward the building. I got about halfway there when Gretchen called. I talked to her for maybe three minutes. Not long. I'm guessing it took five minutes more to get inside the building and up to his office. I saw what I saw and stayed maybe a couple minutes."

"What did you do in his office?" Rosa asked.

"Looked around," I said. "I walked behind his desk to see

what was on his screen. It was a spreadsheet program like the one you have." I nodded at Rosa.

"Excel," Rosa said.

"Yeah," I said. "It didn't mean anything to me. I left. This time, I went down the back stairs and out to the alley."

"Why?" Valerie asked.

"In case someone saw me walk in. I didn't want to give them two opportunities to make me."

"Maybe someone was waiting for you at the front door," Larry said.

"I didn't hear anything," I said. "Maybe someone was, but—" I wanted to say I have a sixth sense about danger but worried it sounded stupid. Gretchen lets me talk all I want about intuition, feelings about negative or positive energy, all that fucking esoteric stuff. Larry rolls his eyes.

"Did you think someone was there? Did you feel any danger?" Rosa knew me.

"No," I said. "I never had a sense of being followed. That day or any day. Also, it would make sense for them to kill me in the dude's office rather than drag my ass back up there. That's unnecessary work and would leave evidence."

"That's true," Larry said. "If it was a murder-suicide or murder-murder plan, someone would have been waiting for you up there. I guess they could have been planning to kill you downstairs, but that'd certainly leave lots of questions. They could have planned to cart you off somewhere, but wouldn't want to leave blood at the scene."

"Best scenario is killing me in his office," I said. What I left unsaid was Rosa or Valerie were the two best suspects for such a scenario.

"I'm the only likely person to do that," Rosa said. "Right? Who else would have a motive?" She shook her head. "It wasn't me."

"Who knows your Saturday schedule?" Larry asked.

Rosa looked at Valerie who shrugged.

"Do you generally do the same thing on Saturday?" Larry asked.

"I guess," Rosa said. "Actually, we don't do much. Sleep in. Do things around the house." She didn't know where Larry was going with this.

"Is there anyone who'd know where you were every Saturday?" he asked. "Absolutely know."

"Besides Valerie," I said.

"We go at work real hard during the week, so, on Saturday we decompress," Rosa said. "Sometimes we don't even go out of the house."

"I'm trying to figure out," Larry said, "who would know it would be difficult for you to establish an alibi on a Saturday. Especially if Valerie wasn't here."

"Oh," Rosa said. She hit her head a few times with her fist, letting us know she was sorry for being so thick-headed. She thought for a moment. "I suppose if someone observed us for a while they might see a pattern."

"In order to expedite this," Larry said, "we should split off and question the two of you separately. Don't take it in any way to mean I suspect either of you."

Rosa shrugged. "Fine," she said. "Let's do it."

Valerie pouted.

"If you don't mind," Larry said to Rosa, "I'll interview you. Kell, you take Valerie."

Larry wanted the opportunity to talk to Rosa alone. She was up for it too. "It'll be my pleasure," Rosa said.

Larry and Rosa had gone from being super-competitive about who trusted me more to falling in love.

On the other hand, Valerie was downright hostile. I motioned her to follow me into the living room and grabbed a legal pad and pen. She reluctantly followed, and we sat on the sofa.

I jotted down questions, eavesdropping on Larry and Rosa's

conversation. He mentioned how he used to play 'a little college football.' He loved to throw it in whenever he could.

Rosa wanted to know where. He told her USC. She told him she'd gone to the University of Chicago. He was, as you can imagine, impressed.

"I got a degree in economics," Rosa said. "And then started my own company. What did you study?" she asked.

"Sociology at USC," Larry said. "I got a masters in criminology at Berkeley."

Color Rosa intrigued. Color Larry smitten. They continued going back and forth, learning nuggets about each other. He hadn't started asking real questions yet. I expected to look over and see Larry on his back with Rosa rubbing his belly.

Valerie was miffed about the whole thing. She made several huffy noises while I worked on writing down the questions.

"Is there anyone you suspect?" I asked.

She shook her head. "No one."

"Can you think about it for at least a second?"

"Believe it or not," Valerie said with heat, "I've been thinking about it since Rosa got the call last night. So, Kell, I have thought about it for much more than a second."

I knew what I wanted to ask, but had to be careful because I didn't want to get slapped in the face again. Gin called it encoding, choosing the best symbols, in this case, words, for Valerie to decode. I wanted to find out if Rosa and Valerie had taken anyone else into their collective bed and fucked her (or their) brains out. I certainly couldn't ask that, could I?

"What?" she asked, impatient with my inability to form a sentence.

"Do you and Rosa, you know, do you guys ever bring anyone else home?"

She was insulted. "No."

"You guys seem to have an open relationship, so—"

"We don't have an open relationship."

"You invited me down here, and—"

"*I* didn't invite you."

I leaned back. Valerie regretted her tone. "This isn't something we normally do. I know what you're asking. You're the only person we've done that with."

On the one hand, I was flattered. On the other hand, I didn't believe her. She must have read my face because she said, "It's true."

"Have you slept with anyone besides Rosa since you met her?" I asked.

She thought for a minute. "Just you."

Larry and Rosa giggled. I have no idea what questions he was asking, but she was thoroughly amused. It wasn't going as well for me.

"If you're holding out on me—"

"I'm not."

"This is important for Rosa, Valerie."

She leaned forward and said through her teeth, "I said only you."

"Have you flirted?"

She gave me a look like she thought I was crazy. "Where is this going?"

"Maybe whoever did it planned it so they could have you."

She shook her head. "That theory doesn't work because there's not another person. Except you."

"What about Dolores?"

Valerie wanted to hit me again. Not desiring another shot in the face, thank you very much, I swerved.

"She's-my-niece," she said.

"Oh."

"What is *wrong* with you?"

"You never told me that."

"I certainly did."

"No. I know you didn't. I definitely would have remembered

that."

"My sister Marian's daughter," Valerie said.

I was afraid to ask about Dana, but felt I had to. "The intern?"

She gave me a 'get real' look. "Dana? She's a college intern. The only other person in this equation is you. Nobody is sleeping with Dolores or Dana."

"You still think it's me?"

Larry and Rosa stopped their love-in, and glanced over at us. Larry gave me a look. He often cautions me to stay cool, not lose my temper. Admittedly, it's one of my weaknesses.

I lowered my voice. "Come on, Valerie. You're gorgeous. You don't expect me to believe that no one has come on to you in the time you've known Rosa."

"I can handle myself. I can't think of anyone who would do this to Rosa."

"What about the marble guy?"

"The marble guy?"

"The guy who—"

She shook her head. "You think I'm having an affair with Jeff?"

"He notices you when he's here."

"He looks at you too. And Rosa. He's a guy."

"Think, Valerie. Anyone from your past? You've lived in Miami before, right?"

"Yes. We don't have enemies. I suppose there are competitors, but that's true in any business. You seem to be looking for some romantic competitor. There's no one. And, anyway, it doesn't matter what I say because you don't believe me."

"It's not like you believe me either. Do you honestly think I would come here, enjoy the hospitality, and then set up Rosa?"

"I'm saying *you're* the most likely suspect."

"And I'm saying *you're* the most likely suspect."

Rosa and Larry were watching us. They looked like a married couple, leaning towards each other, heads almost touching.

"How's it going?" Larry asked.

I made a frustrated noise. Valerie leaned back against her chair.

It wasn't going well.

EIGHTEEN

"We'll try something else," Larry said. "Now, understand, I'm not accusing anyone of being a liar."

We stared at him. I was as clueless as Rosa and Valerie about what he was cooking up.

"There's something I'd like to try," he said.

We waited. Valerie stared at him like he had three heads. Rosa motioned with her hands for him to bring it on.

Larry opened up his satchel and rooted around before pulling out a small black-and-white gadget. I had an idea what it was and laughed.

"Since you find this so funny, Kell, you can go first," he said.

"You're joking," I said.

"I'm not," Larry said.

He waved at me to come to him. I made a face.

"What is it?" Rosa asked, leaning forward to get a better look.

"A lie detector machine," Larry said.

Rosa threw back her head and laughed. "You are too much, Larry."

Larry had told me about it before, but I'd never seen it. He'd said he was glad that Gin didn't know he had one because she'd whip it out on a daily basis. Thank God Gretchen didn't know a home model existed, or I'd be done for sure.

"Kell," Larry said, beckoning me with his finger.

I sat down at the table in the chair next to him and shot him a 'Are you sure you want to do this' look.

"How does it work?" Rosa asked.

Larry held it up, so Rosa could see it.

The machine was the size of a hand-held computer game, about nine inches long, six inches wide, and two inches thick.

"De-Fib-ulator," Rosa read.

"For God's sake," Valerie muttered.

Rosa flashed a huge smile. "That's wild," she said. "Does it work?"

"You think something with the name De-Fib-ulator actually works?" Valerie asked her.

Rosa ignored her question and looked at Larry.

"It's amazingly accurate for what it is," Larry said. "I've used ones that sold for thousands. This one comes close."

"Give me a break," Valerie said. She crossed her legs and folded her hands.

"How does it work?" Rosa asked, reaching out her palm.

Larry handed it to her. "I ask three yes-no questions to get a baseline reading. Then I ask the real questions."

"What does it do if you're lying?" Rosa asked, scrutinizing it.

Larry hesitated. He didn't want to tell her. I snickered.

"Tell her," I said.

"What?" Rosa looked from me to Larry.

"Well, it's not real scientific, Rosa," he said. "This character's face comes up. Fellow by the name of Demonochio. If you're lying—"

"Yes?" Rosa asked.

"His nose and horns grow," Larry said.

Valerie made a disgusted sound. Rosa chuckled with delight. "We need to get one of these, Val."

"Maybe you should take it," Valerie suggested to Larry,

scowling. "How do we know we can trust you?"

"Sure," he said. "If you want to question me later, I don't have a problem with it. I'll show you how it works. Nothing's admissible, of course, but let's see what happens."

"You can get a false positive, can't you?" Valerie asked.

Larry shrugged. "I'm trained in how to use this. The more experience you have with it, the better the results."

Valerie still didn't buy it, but Rosa was curious. She handed the machine back to Larry.

"I'll ask baseline questions first," Larry said to me.

"Go ahead," I said.

"Is your name Kelleher Digby?" he asked.

"Yes."

"Do you live in Stone Mountain, Georgia?"

"Yes."

"Are you over forty years of age?"

"No," I said.

The room grew quiet. "Okay," Larry said.

"Did you frame Rosa for the murder of Herb Martinez?" he asked.

"No."

"Did you kill Herb Martinez?"

"No."

"Do you know who did?"

"No."

"Thank you, Kell," Larry said. "No deception." He held up the machine for everyone to see. "Rosa."

Rosa leaned back and folded her hands.

"You're not doing this, are you?" Valerie asked her.

"It said Kell didn't lie?" Rosa asked.

"No deception," Larry said. "None."

Rosa's face turned serious. "I'll tell you right now, Larry, I won't lie. If it comes back and says I'm lying—"

"Nothing is one hundred percent accurate," Larry said.

"You're obviously under lots of stress right now. Just give it a try. I'll start with three baseline questions.

"Is your last name Gold?"

"Yes."

"Do you live in Miami?"

"Yes."

"Did you ever try to have Kell killed?"

Rosa shot a look at me. "You told him," she accused.

"No," I said, looking at Larry. "I never told anyone."

"I guessed," he said. Larry kept his eyes on the little machine.

"It's complicated," Rosa said.

"Yes or no," Larry said.

Rosa sighed. "Yes." She was shook up. "It's a long story. It's not totally what it sounds like."

"We'll talk about it later," Larry said. "Did you try to have her killed when you ordered the hit on Herb Martinez?"

"No," Rosa said.

"Do you believe Kell set you up on Herb Martinez's murder?"

Rosa looked at me, Larry, and finally at Valerie. She didn't want to answer. "Yes."

"Rosa, I didn't," I said.

Larry held up a hand, motioning me to be quiet. Fuck him.

Rosa didn't look at me. "Larry, my boy, you're giving me a lot harder time than you gave Kell."

"Just seems that way, Rosa," Larry said. "Do you know who killed Herb Martinez?"

"No," Rosa said. "What does it say?"

Rosa tried to look at the machine. Larry shielded it from her.

"Did it say I lied about anything?" she asked.

"The only time it showed deception was on the question about whether you ever tried to kill Kell," he said.

I had no idea if Larry was telling the truth. We'd talk about it later.

"By the way, I'm real interested in hearing that story," Larry said.

"How does it work?" Rosa asked. "It must be something with the voice, right?"

Larry nodded. "There are changes in the voice when people try to deceive. Valerie."

She shook her head. "This whole thing has already made me nervous. The results won't be any good. It'll show up in my voice."

Everyone looked at her. "I know what the truth is," she said, "but I'm a nervous wreck." She pointed to the machine. "I'll come off as a liar on everything."

We waited. Valerie knew as well as we did that she didn't have a choice. Not after Rosa and I were tested.

"Come on, Val," Rosa said. "Do it and get it over with. No one will think you're lying if it—"

Yeah, right. Reluctantly, Valerie nodded for Larry to begin.

"Is your name Valerie?" he asked.

"Yes."

"Do you live in Miami?"

"Yes," Valerie said.

"Do you work in real estate?"

"Yes."

"Did you frame Rosa in Herb Martinez's murder?"

"No."

Larry looked at the machine and twisted his mouth. Valerie sat up and tried to see the machine's screen.

"Did you take any actions that led to the police suspecting Rosa?" Larry asked.

"No."

"Do you know who killed Herb Martinez?" he asked.

"No."

Larry stared at the machine.

"Well?" Valerie asked. "Did I pass?"

I watched Rosa. I wanted Larry to ask her, "Do you have any doubts about Valerie?" Actually, I didn't need a lie detector to know the answer to that. Rosa was anxious to hear what Larry had to say.

"No deception," he said.

Valerie breathed out. So did Rosa.

"One last thing, Valerie," Larry said.

The room went silent.

"Were you part of any conspiracy to have Kell killed?" he asked.

Valerie looked at Rosa. Rosa started to say something. Larry held up his hand to silence her. Valerie looked at me. I thought she might start crying. She shook her head like a kid who'd gotten caught doing something bad. Larry waited, holding the machine toward her.

"Valerie," he said. "Yes or no."

"Yes," she said, lowering her eyes.

"Was it part of the Herb Martinez hit?" he asked.

Her eyes shot back up. "No."

"Larry," Rosa said. "Can I say something?"

"Go ahead," he said.

I couldn't wait to hear this.

"It was in Atlanta," Rosa said. "I guess Kell told you part of it."

He shook his head.

"I never said a word," I said.

"Valerie never felt right about it," Rosa said. "It was my idea. It was a bad one."

"You're talking about something that happened in Atlanta?" Larry asked.

Rosa nodded. "Years ago."

"You didn't try to kill Kell in Miami?" he asked Valerie.

"Absolutely not," she said. She pointed to the machine. "That thing is a liar if it says I did."

"It says you're telling the truth," Larry said. "Like I said, ladies, that Atlanta thing is a story I want to hear." He pointed to Rosa. "You and I need to talk some more. Kell, finish your interview with Valerie."

Yeah, whatever. I had something else on my mind. When Larry wasn't looking—he was so fucking focused on Rosa—I snatched the De-Fib-ulator and motioned Valerie to follow me into the living room.

We sat on the couch. Valerie folded her hands together. I pulled up my feet and sat cross-legged.

"Let's have some fun with this thing," I said.

NINETEEN

I'd watched Larry, so I knew how the machine worked. At least well enough. Larry would have insisted I read the fucking instructions, but fuck that.

"What's your last name anyway?" I asked Valerie. "Is it Bach?"

"Bach." She pronounced it like an NPR announcer.

"Okay. Is your name Valerie Bach?" I played along and mimicked her exaggerated pronunciation.

"Yes," Valerie said, "but I don't think we should be playing with this thing."

"Yeah. Okay. Do you live in Miami?"

"Yes."

"Are you in love with Rosa?"

"Yes. Kell, I really—"

"Okay. Did you ever fall for me?"

Valerie gave me a look. "Come on. Don't do this." She moved her head, so she could see into the kitchen. I leaned back and looked in too. Rosa and Larry were involved in an intense conversation. If you'd seen them in a restaurant, you'd think they were adulterous lovers meeting on the sly.

"You can ask me anything when it's your turn," I said. "Come on, Valerie, quit being a fucking baby and answer the question."

She sighed and tilted her head to the side. "Yes."

This surprised me. I looked down at the machine. The bitch was telling the truth. It'd been so long since I'd blushed I wasn't sure what the odd feeling in my face was.

"Which time?" I asked. "Atlanta or here?"

Now she fucking blushed. "Both."

"You're a liar." I looked down at the machine. My mouth dropped open.

"Give me that thing," she said, grabbing it out of my hands. I smiled and squinted.

"You're so fucking full of yourself, Kell."

Valerie leaned forward and asked her questions quickly.

"Is your name Kell Digby?" she asked.

"Yes."

"Do you live in Georgia?"

"Yes."

"Is Larry your brother-in-law?"

"Yes."

"Did you and Rosa have sex when you did the California scam?"

Whoa. "This is bad idea," I said, reaching for the machine. Valerie pulled it away. I glanced over at Rosa again. She had no idea Valerie and I were playing Truth or Dare. I tried to catch Larry's eye. Maybe he could get me out of this. Nothing doing. They were intrigued with each, way too engrossed to pay us any mind. If Larry were a lesbian, or Rosa were straight, we'd never see the two of them again.

"No," I said.

She looked down at the machine. "Wow. His nose really does grow." Her shoulders sagged. "I thought so. Did she have sex with you here when I was at the hospital?"

"No."

Valerie looked at the machine. "Good." She met my eyes. "Are you in love with me?"

I'd asked myself that very same question a few times. I had fallen for her in Atlanta when she and Rosa tricked me. Of course, I got over it real quick when she tried to kill me. Here in Miami, things had been good, and I wondered a few times if I wasn't falling again.

"Hey, ladies, that's not a parlor game," Larry called over to us.

We both had guilty faces.

"What are they doing?" Rosa asked. She walked over and held out her hand. Valerie gave the detector to her. "What did you guys ask each other?"

We shook our heads and peeled off to the patio, shut the glass door behind us and quietly, awkwardly sat at the wrought iron table for a few minutes.

"We need to talk, don't you think?" Valerie finally asked.

Straight ahead of me was the rectangular pool. Beyond it was a brick wall with blooming plants and a gushing water feature that emptied into the pool. I had a pool in Georgia and wondered how expensive it'd be to make it like Rosa's.

"We probably should have done this a long time ago," Valerie said.

"You go first," I said.

"I never wanted to do what Rosa and I planned back in Atlanta," Valerie said. "I'm not putting it on her, but it was a stupid idea. It was never something that I wanted to be part of it. I've done things, sure, but nothing like that. It's important you know that. I'm not saying I would have left Rosa or anything like that, but I didn't like how things ended. It didn't feel right. I know you worked things out with Rosa, but I never felt like you and I did."

I shrugged. For all I knew, Valerie was playing me again. It was easy.

"You didn't kill me, and you could have," Valerie said.

"I was never hired to kill you. I'm a professional."

"Yeah. You chose not to. You also didn't hurt Rosa."

"Don't be too hard on her about us hooking up back in Atlanta after the California thing. She felt sorry for me. I was pathetic." If I remembered correctly, Rosa told me that Valerie knew about it and was cool. Not that my memory could be trusted, but it seemed like she told me she and Valerie had discussed it.

"I suspected it," she said.

"Did you ask her?"

"I gave her the opportunity to tell me."

Whatever the hell that meant. "Did you guys talk about bringing me here specifically to take out Martinez?" I asked. I had the opportunity to delve further and took it.

"She told me you were going through a breakup," Valerie said. "She was worried you might do something stupid."

"Kill myself?"

"No. Just general stupid. She thought we'd have some fun if you came down here."

"What did you think?"

"It took me a while to warm up to the idea," Valerie said. "For one thing, I didn't know how you felt about me after what happened."

"Did you specifically talk about Martinez?"

Valerie looked puzzled. "I can't remember. I don't think so."

I wished I had the De-Fib-ulator back.

"There was no definite plan," she said. "We talked about seeing if you'd work for us."

"Doing what?"

"Different things," Valerie said. "Whatever turned out to be a good fit. She wanted someone she trusted."

"What about messing around? Did you guys talk about that?"

"Not in those words. We were in the mode of, 'Let's see what happens.' I have to tell you, Kell, I got scared when Rosa was framed. I thought you did it because you wanted to be with me.

Sorry if that makes me sound conceited. That's why I got hostile with you. I got her worked up too. I'm sorry."

"You trust me now?"

"The De-Fib says you're telling the truth." Valerie smiled.

"What do you think of Larry?" I asked.

"If he were a woman, I'd be worried."

I glanced inside the window. Rosa and Larry were still seated at the table, immersed in their discussion.

"Rosa is fascinated by him," Valerie said. "I've never seen her react this way to a guy."

"He's a bright guy," I said. "Brilliant might be a better word."

"He seems to be. You didn't answer my question. I answered yours. Come on. Be fair."

I slid my hand across the table until our fingertips touched. "Yes."

"Let's go back in," Valerie said. "I'll make something to eat." She didn't wait for my answer and hurried to the sliding glass door.

"You guys getting hungry?" Valerie asked a little too loudly, when we stepped inside.

"We were just talking about food," Rosa said. "Can you make something Cuban?"

Valerie looked at Larry. "How about black beans, fish, rice, fried plantains?"

"Sounds great," he said.

Valerie, knowing what she was looking for, pulled several pans out of the cupboards. Larry excused himself.

Rosa motioned me to follow her to the living room. "What did you ask Valerie on that machine?" she whispered.

"It wasn't appropriate," I said. "I shouldn't have asked."

"Yeah, but what was it?"

"If she'd ever been in love with me."

"Oh." Rosa thought about it for a moment. "What'd she say?"

"She said no."

"Sweetie," Rosa scolded. "Don't lie to me." She rolled her eyes. "I know you both too well. What did she ask you?"

"If you and I had sex when we went to California."

Rosa thought for a moment. "We didn't actually do it in California."

"That's not how she phrased it."

"You told her."

"I told her we didn't."

Rosa chuckled. "And you failed the test. Let me ask you something."

"Please don't get that detector."

"I don't need the De-Fib with you, sweetie. Did you know we'd all end up in bed when you came down here?"

"I thought you and I might. But, no, I never expected what happened."

"Have you thought about moving here?"

"I have. I don't think it's a good idea."

"You're probably right."

"I'm still hoping Gretchen will come back."

"Larry said she's a great girl. Really good for you. He said she's nurturing. Takes good care of you. He thinks I'm a bad influence."

"Why would he think that?"

Rosa smiled. "If you weren't with Gretchen, would you consider getting back with me?"

"We were never really together."

"You know what I mean."

"Probably," I said. "I don't see it happening, though, because you and Larry have fallen in love."

"Yes. He's dreamy. Do you think he'll figure out what's going on with Martinez?"

I nodded.

"I wish he'd been here earlier," Rosa said. "He's right about the attorney. I was out of my league." She paused for a moment. "Larry can't stay long. Your sister keeps him on a short leash. Do you think I could talk him into moving here?"

"Absolutely not."

"I didn't think so."

"You're not moving Larry into your bedroom tonight, are you?"

"I've already told him that he can have the guest room in the other wing," she said. "It's got a nice view of the courtyard. He'll like it. He's coming in to work with us tomorrow."

This was news to me.

"I don't suppose you two are close enough that you share a bedroom," Rosa said.

"He snores," I said.

She leaned in. "So do you, sweetie."

Just at that moment, Larry walked back in the room. He abruptly stopped, turned, and walked back where he came from.

"Larry, it's cool," I said.

He tentatively turned.

"I'll help Valerie in the kitchen," Rosa said. "I'm sure you two want to put your heads together anyway."

Larry waited until she disappeared into the kitchen before he motioned me to him. I figured he had some news.

"I'm confused," Larry said. "The chemistry is odd. I can't figure it out. Which one is your ex?"

I tilted my head. "Both."

He wasn't expecting this. "Both? At separate times?" he asked.

That was a hard one to answer. "Sort of."

He pointed at me and then to the kitchen. "So what's going on now?"

I raised my eyebrows. He raised his. I nodded.

"No way," he said.

"Up until the day of the hit."

A wave of envy crossed his face. He moved his hand in space. "All three of you?"

"Yes."

"Lesbians are God's chosen people," Larry said. "My God, Kell."

"Snap out of it, Larry. Listen. Rosa said you're coming into work with her tomorrow. What's your plan?"

"Before we move on, please tell me it wasn't as good as you thought it'd be. That the fantasy in your head was better than reality."

I stared at him a long time.

"Wow. Unfuckingbelievable. Whose idea was it?" he asked.

"Probably Rosa's. She pulls everyone's strings."

"That woman is a fucking genius," he said. "If Gretchen comes back, what will you tell her?"

I laughed. "Nothing. You think I'm nuts. No fucking way. The last time I talked to her was last night. Right before Rosa got the phone call from her lawyer. She hasn't called back."

"Did you argue?" he asked.

"Not really. It was tense, uncomfortable. Who is she seeing?"

He shook his head. "I don't want any part of this."

"It's Michelle, isn't it?" That had been my guess all along. Gretchen had dated Michelle before she met me. They'd break up and get back together. One of those. Gretchen broke off all contact with her after we got involved. I hadn't thought any more about her. I mean, who the fuck cares? Her loss was my gain, and all that. But knowing Gretchen, I could see her contacting her again in Oceanvue.

"The only thing I know," he said, "is that Gin isn't crazy about her. Whatever that means."

"She's not crazy about me right now either. By the way, where did you tell her you were?"

"St. Louis," he said. "For an emergency consultation. Anyway, yes, I want all of us to go in tomorrow."

"You know what you're looking for."

"I've got a good idea."

"What do you want me to do tomorrow?"

"Run interference for me," Larry said. "Let me do my thing without anyone knowing what I'm doing."

We got called to dinner. Everyone did a good job of avoiding unpleasant talk. Rosa and Larry carried the conversation. Rosa had purchased a wine from a local restaurant and was hot for Larry to try it.

I don't give a fuck about wine, so I talked to Valerie about the meal. She'd put fish in everyone else's dinner but made me a vegetarian plate. That was thoughtful.

Near the end of dinner, after Valerie brought out chocolate cake, she announced that Uncle Buddy was doing much better and planned to take off the next week to recuperate. The test results showed a minor heart attack—his third in the last two years—and his doctor wanted him to stay in bed a while.

"I'll try to get an appointment with the lawyer tomorrow afternoon, Larry," Rosa said, when there was a lull.

"I'm sure she'll see you," he said. "I've given her a heads up."

Rosa appreciated that Larry was on it. "Valerie's taking off early in the afternoon to see Uncle Buddy and Aunt Marie," she said. "Dana will be gone, too, so it'll be just you and Dolores in the afternoon."

Larry nodded. "I want to get a feel for the place, look through records. I also need to make some phone calls."

"What exactly do you do, Larry?" Valerie asked.

It wasn't an appropriate question. The table remained silent.

"Sorry," Valerie said.

"It's difficult to explain," Larry said.

Valerie put up her hands, letting him know he didn't have to answer.

"In some ways, it's like a detective agency," he said. "In fact, I've thought about starting a real agency."

"I can see that," Rosa said. She probably thought it'd be a good front.

"Kell could be part of it," he said.

We'd joked about starting a detective agency, but I didn't know he was serious.

"When she was young, we talked about her going into law enforcement," Rosa said.

Larry chuckled.

"We really did," she said.

It was true. I'm not sure what we were thinking, but Rosa even signed me up for criminology classes.

"She would have made a good FBI agent," Rosa said. "We also thought about Secret Service."

"It was mostly Rosa," I said. I stopped taking classes after Rosa recruited me to work for Ironclad.

"I'm thinking of doing something different," Larry said. "It's probably time." He meant he feared Gin would be on to him soon.

Rosa nodded. "Everything is more difficult now. Major cities have video cameras everywhere." She looked at me. "Chicago is loaded with them."

Rosa turned her attention to Larry. "Can you figure this out?" she asked, looking vulnerable. It might have been an act, but she sold it. Larry brought out something in her I didn't see often. Their chemistry wasn't entirely sexual, though there was some of that too. It was the way their minds interacted, the way they delighted in each other's thoughts.

"Every human puzzle is solvable," Larry said. "Someone did something, and they did it for a reason."

TWENTY

We sat around and yakked after dinner. I knew damn well it wouldn't turn into a love fest with Larry there. It was okay. Rosa, Valerie, and I hadn't slept much the previous night.

I yawned. When Rosa shielded one too, I made eye contact with Larry.

"I'm tucking Larry in," I said.

Everyone said good night. Larry got hugs from Valerie and Rosa. I got friendly kisses.

I led Larry to his room. My plan was to immediately go to bed, but I spied the De-Fib-ulator on the dresser.

"No," he said, when I picked it up, "we're not playing with that damn thing. By the way, I snowed them on its reliability."

"What are you afraid of, Larry?" I turned on the machine. "Is your name Larry Howell?"

He sighed. "Yes."

"Are you married to Gin?"

"Yes."

"Do you live in California?"

"Yes."

"Have you ever cheated on Gin?" I asked.

Larry put up his hands. "I don't want to do this, Kell. I told you the results aren't reliable."

"Yeah, yeah, yeah."

He leaned forward. "No. I have never cheated on her. How did you meet Rosa?"

I shook the machine and frowned. "You're messing up the results. She was my babysitter."

This silenced him for a moment. "That explains a lot," he finally said.

"Nah, it wasn't like that, Larry. She was a nice Jewish girl. We hooked up after I grew up."

"Is she bi?" he asked.

I wanted to slap him. I knew what his dirty mind was thinking. I balled up my fist.

"Calm down, Kell. I'm just asking."

"No," I said. "She's not bi."

"It was just in my head. I was never doing anything. Honest to God."

"Have you ever cheated on Gin?" I pointed the machine at him.

"*No.*"

I placed the machine back on the dresser. "We need to figure out who wants what Rosa has."

"I have to put a spin on this because I need to get back home before Gin starts to wonder," Larry said.

"You have a feeling, don't you?"

"So do you," he said.

"It'll kill Rosa."

"We're not there yet, Kell."

I nodded. We might not be there, but we were close.

"I want you to go with Rosa to meet Sylvia," he said. "She never should have seen the other guy. I'm surprised they haven't gotten search warrants yet."

"For here?"

"And her office downtown," Larry said.

"You think something's been planted?"

"I'm working off-balance on this one, Kell. I don't know. I

do know she'll freak out if they tear her place apart."

"You should have seen her last night, Larry," I whispered. "Total, complete meltdown."

He raised his eyebrows.

"I've never seen her like that," I said. "It was a horror movie."

I got the idea he would have liked to have seen it.

I slept better. I was disappointed that Gretchen hadn't called, but it was just as well. I was working a job, and she distracts me. I needed to keep my focus.

All of us left the house at the same time for the office building. Valerie drove alone in her Lexus SUV. Larry took my Mustang, and I rode with Rosa in her Jaguar.

I hung out with Larry while Rosa and Valerie followed their normal routine. I learned a lot from Larry about how to unravel the mystery we were looking at. He showed me how to read Excel spreadsheets and what to look for in a company's books. I also listened in on his phone calls. I doubted I could do what he did, but I definitely wanted him on my side.

Rosa scheduled an appointment for one p.m. with attorney Sylvia Wright. Larry intimated to me a couple times that Sylvia was a dragon lady. I wasn't in a hurry to meet her.

Larry, Rosa, Valerie, and I met for lunch at a diner just down the street from the office building. While finishing up our sandwiches, Larry cleared his throat. Bad news was coming. He was considerate enough to wait until Rosa finished her chicken salad sandwich.

"Rosa," he said, "Sylvia Wright is a real bitch. She's got no warmth, and she'll hurt your feelings."

"Want me to go with you?" Valerie whispered to Rosa.

Rosa shook her head. "Kell's coming with me. It'll be okay. Thanks for telling me, Larry. I'm a big girl." She wasn't convincing. After a short pause, she added, "I assume she's worth the trouble."

"Absolutely," Larry said. "She's also expensive."

Rosa waved her hand. "You said she's the best. That's what I want."

Yes, that's what Rosa wanted, but on the way to Sylvia's downtown office her breathing was labored like a COPD patient. I was behind the wheel because Rosa was too nervous to drive. I asked her to sit back and relax. She didn't sit back. She didn't relax. I wasn't exactly a fountain of calmness myself. We snapped back and forth. She didn't like my driving. I didn't like her nitpicking.

We finally arrived at the sleek cylindrical skyscraper in the Brickell neighborhood fifteen minutes early. Rosa instructed me to drive around the block. I wasn't in the mood, so I pulled into the parking garage.

"We'll wait in the car," I said. "I'm not driving around the fucking block in this fucking traffic." It probably doesn't sound like it, but my tone was gentle.

She exhaled hard. "I'm glad you're with me," she said, clutching my hand.

We stared at the clock in silence until Rosa spoke again. "I'm scared to death of this woman. What am I so afraid of?"

I didn't have any answers. "She's just a woman, Rosa," I said.

Four minutes before our appointment, we got out of the car and made our way into the building. Sylvia's office was on the thirty-eighth floor. We arrived on her floor at 12:58 PM. and easily found her suite. It oozed money, but in an elegant way. Still, I couldn't ditch the idea that Rosa and I were on our way to see the principal in the most expensive school in the world. I'd been to detention a few times in high school, so I wasn't as scared as Miss Valedictorian.

The receptionist was sexy in a classy way. We introduced ourselves, she called Ms. Wright's office, and a tall, well-dressed woman came out to greet us. We re-introduced ourselves. She shook our hands, smiled, and motioned us to follow her. This, I thought, can't be the dragon lady. It wasn't. The polite lady led us down a thickly carpeted hallway lined with dark paneling and wall sconces. She opened the door at the hallway's end and stepped back. We were expected to walk in. Rosa froze. I thought about pushing her, but instead walked in first.

The office was huge. It took me some time to locate the desk and Sylvia Wright. She didn't smile, but stood and motioned us to sit in two white high-back upholstered chairs a few feet from her desk. The chairs probably cost a thousand apiece.

Behind Sylvia, framed in floor-to-ceiling glass, was the cityscape. It gave the impression that Sylvia owned the city. Maybe she did.

Sylvia was about sixty years old, five feet tall, one hundred pounds. Her dark black dyed hair was cut like a helmet. She reached across the desk and shook both of our hands, and then sat down and pointed at Rosa.

"You're Rosa Gold," she said in a New Jersey accent. I don't know what it is about a New Jersey accent, but it always sounds like someone wants to start something. Sylvia turned her attention to me. "Who the hell are you?" she asked.

Before I could open my mouth, Rosa said, "She's my bodyguard."

I shot a sidelong glance at Rosa. She avoided my gaze.

Sylvia looked me up and down and folded her hands on her desk. "All right," she said. "My next question is why do you think you need a bodyguard in my office?"

Rosa's usually smooth, but this one threw her. "Do you want her to leave?" she asked in a small voice.

We hadn't been in Sylvia Wright's office a minute, and Rosa had already thrown me under the bus.

"She can stay," Sylvia said. "But I didn't ask you *what* she was. I asked *who* she was."

"I'm Kelleher Digby." Rosa's weak demeanor freaked me out. One of us had to act confident.

"Sounds like a law firm, Ms. Digby," Sylvia said. I got the feeling that she was playing with me. I didn't know if she was playing with me because she liked me or didn't like me. I'd keep my mouth shut until I knew.

Sylvia played rough with Rosa. "Ms. Gold, you got yourself in a pickle when you talked to the police. What were you thinking? Don't answer that. You weren't thinking. You don't strike me as an idiot, Ms. Gold, so stop acting like one."

She waited for Rosa to say something. Rosa wisely kept her mouth shut. I had the feeling that whatever you said, Sylvia would shut you down—and fucking fast.

"Just so you both know," Sylvia said, "if you get in trouble in the future, get in touch with a criminal lawyer, not a real estate lawyer. I can probably get your interview thrown out if it comes to that. Based on incompetence. Not yours, but the attorney's."

Wow. I've never heard anyone even hint Rosa was incompetent. I glanced over, wondering how she was taking it. Rosa was wide-eyed, white-faced, and white-knuckled. Her hands grasped her white Chanel purse.

"Meanwhile," Sylvia continued, "you will have no more coffee klatches with the police. Also, if you decide you want me to represent you, you need to understand that I'm extremely unlikely to look for a plea deal."

"I don't want one," Rosa said. "I didn't do it."

Sylvia stared at her a long time. When she continued, it was like she hadn't heard Rosa. "Some lawyers specialize in that. I don't deal. If you're looking for that, you should look for different representation."

"Larry said you were the best," Rosa said. "You're the expert. I'll do whatever you say." She tried not to sound desperate, but that's exactly what she sounded like.

Instinctively, I put my hand over her shaking ones. They felt ice cold and hard, like a frozen fish.

Sylvia watched and tilted her head, like she was thinking. "Larry Howell is a prince," she said, almost daring us to disagree. We didn't.

"He's my brother-in-law," I said.

Sylvia again tilted her head, like she was figuring out a puzzle or decoding a word scramble.

"I need you to sign an agreement," Sylvia said. "Ms. Gold, my assistant Gayla Armen will explain it to you." Sylvia pressed a button on her desktop. "Gayla, Ms. Gold is ready to go over the terms with you." Within seconds, the door opened. A different tall beauty swept in, smiling and cheerful. Rosa stood. I followed her lead.

"Ms. Digby," Sylvia said, "if you don't mind, I'd like to talk to you for a few minutes. You can meet Ms. Gold in the reception room after we've finished."

I sat. Ms. Gold didn't look back. Rosa couldn't get out of Sylvia's office fast enough. The door closed.

"So you're a bodyguard?" Sylvia asked.

Rosa and I should have gotten our script straight before we met with Sylvia.

"Yes, ma'am," I said. Even after moving to the south, I'm not someone who ma'am's a lot. I thought I should in this situation.

"Here in Miami?" Sylvia asked.

"Actually, I live in Georgia. I—"

She stared at me. When I say stared, I mean bitch didn't blink.

"I'm not really a full-time bodyguard," I said. "I used to be, but right now I'm just helping out Rosa."

"You two have a personal relationship?"

"And professional. I worked for her as a bodyguard when she owned a company in Chicago."

"You were her bodyguard in Chicago?"

"No. I was a bodyguard for her company. She supplied

bodyguards." And hit men. I probably shouldn't bring that up, right?

"Do you think she needs a bodyguard here?" Sylvia asked.

"Probably not in your office, but someone framed her. That concerns me."

"I'm not giving you a hard time, honey." Honey? I certainly hoped this didn't turn into another Debra situation. I had enough problems. "I might need your services."

I raised my eyebrows. She laughed. "Not me personally," she said. "I'm sure there are people who want to kill me, but no one has the guts. Plus, I have my own personal bodyguard." I didn't know what the fuck she was talking about. Everything she said sounded like an in-joke, but I was clueless. "What I'm asking is, do you freelance?" she asked.

I nodded, not knowing what else to do. I didn't get why she might be pulling me into a trap, but there was something that felt trappish.

"I assume you've had training," she said, "can shoot, have a permit, and so on."

I nodded again. "I'm a little rusty," I confessed, afraid she'd call my bluff.

"It wouldn't take long to get you back up to speed, would it? Most of what I'd want you for is more of the babysitting variety. Not so much protecting the President of the United States."

That was a fucking relief.

"Write down your phone number, so I'll have it," she said. "It won't be a problem to fly you from Georgia?"

I shook my head. She passed a piece of paper and a pen across the desk. I wrote my name and phone number and passed it back.

"Do you work through Ms. Gold?" she asked.

"No. Well—" I thought for a moment. It occurred to me that Rosa might be thinking about changing careers again. It'd be fairly easy to go back into doing what she'd done in the past. "I'm not really sure how it'll work out."

"I see. I'm thrilled you came with her today. I have a feeling that you and I will be great friends."

"Uh-huh."

I shook Sylvia's hand and got the hell out of her office. Rosa was cooling her heels in the reception area. She looked relieved to see me.

"Wow," she said, when we stepped on the elevator. "That woman is intimidating."

We got the giggles when the door closed.

"She offered me a possible job," I said.

Rosa grabbed my arm. "To do what?"

"Did you think she was flirting with me?"

"*Yes.*"

I laughed. "To be a bodyguard."

"Is that a euphemism?"

"I have no fucking idea. When I see Larry, I'll be like, 'Larry, what the fuck?' You feel better about everything?"

"I do," she said. "I had to write a huge check. I will gladly write a bigger one if she gets me out of this."

TWENTY-ONE

"How'd it go?" Larry asked Rosa, when we entered the house.

I was surprised he was already back.

"Fine," Rosa said. "She's my lawyer now."

"Good," he said. "You won't regret it."

"How'd you do?" Rosa asked.

"I'll have something for you tonight. A couple more things I need to check out."

"Really? That quickly?" Rosa was surprised. She looked at me and then back at Larry.

"Kell," Larry said. "I need to talk to Rosa for a few minutes."

I walked out to the pool. The thing about Larry is that he's proven himself right most of the time. However he wants to work something is all right with me. The only time I question him are instances like when he wants me to go by Mabel. Things like that.

I was outside for ten minutes before he joined me.

"Larry, you forgot to mention that Sylvia is a dyke," I said, when he came out.

"You think everyone's gay, don't you? You're not her type. I am."

"You?"

"Don't be so shocked."

I shook my head. "My gaydar must be off."

"She's married."

"Okay."

"To a dude. Who looks like me. Big, handsome guy. Seriously, he's about twenty years younger than her and former law enforcement."

"I can't see it."

"He's her third husband," Larry said, "but they've been together for a while. Did she play rough with Rosa?"

"Yes, and she kept me after school."

"What'd you do?"

"Nothing. I thought she was sweet on me. She asked if I'd work for her."

"Doing what?" he asked.

"Freelance bodyguard slash babysitting. Rosa introduced me as her bodyguard."

"I don't know what to say, Kell. You must have impressed her."

"You know me."

"Are you taking the job?"

"Told her I'd think about it. Why not? Right?"

"It'd be easy work for you," he said.

"Is she a bad guy?"

"Nobody's perfect, but for a lawyer she's ethical. For a lawyer."

"You find out anything more?"

"I've been productive," he said. "Look, I need to ask you a huge favor. Feel free to decline. I mean it."

He'd come all the way to Miami to help me out. I'd be a jackass if I didn't return the favor.

"I have a meeting with the hit man," Larry said.

"How'd you manage that?"

"Magic. Anyway, no offense, but I don't trust his kind. I'd appreciate it if you'd back me up. I'm not brave enough to go there alone without a gun. Will you come with me?"

"Absolutely." I kept a stone face. I'm never sure when Larry's pulling my leg. "What does he think the meeting's about?"

"A hit," he said. "Once we get there, we'll ask some questions, but if he refuses to tell us, that's it."

I thought about it. Would I give up the name of a client?

"How much are you offering him?" I asked.

"Rosa's authorized fifty thousand."

"Wow." Would I take it? I couldn't make a decision like that on my own. I'd consult Rosa. Knowing Rosa, she'd tell me to give up the name. A paying client is a paying client, after all. Fortunately, nothing like this has ever come up.

"What do you know about him?" I asked.

"His name. I have a phone number. It didn't go to him directly. He called me back."

"How did you get this, Larry?"

"Through contacts. Narrowing it down."

Larry knew lots of people, both good and bad.

"I also found out something else interesting," he said. "There are three people who are willing to testify that they witnessed Rosa entering and exiting Martinez's building around the time he was killed."

"They're lying."

"Well paid liars, no doubt." He scrunched up his face. "Another thing. I've asked Rosa not to tell Valerie about our meeting."

Larry and I drove to a nondescript beige brick condo complex on the outskirts of Miami. We passed a wood sign with Beach Oaks Condominiums written in fancy script.

"We're not walking into something, are we, Larry?" I asked in the parking lot.

"A friend vouched for me. We'll see how it goes."

I touched the gun hiding in the pocket of Rosa's black leather jacket. Yeah, it was too warm to be wearing a leather jacket, but fuck that.

I was on edge. I'd never met another hit man. At least that I knew of. Valerie doesn't count because she sucked at it.

"Here's how it'll go," Larry said. "He thinks we're here to talk about a hit. We'll exchange pleasantries, blah, blah, blah. Then I'll tell him we have a deal for him, but there won't be any hurt feelings if he doesn't take it."

"Is that when he shoots us?"

"Put yourself in his position, Kell. What would you do?"

"Hear it out."

"We'll be okay unless he's in love with the person who took out the contract."

The condo building was the kind where everyone had their own exterior front door. We went to one of the back units and made sure we had the right house number.

"Well, here goes," I said.

Larry shifted the handle of the tan briefcase that held the money from his right hand to his left and then rang the bell.

A slight dude answered. I didn't think he was the hit man. He wore khakis and a light blue polo shirt that matched his eye color. He looked to be about thirty, medium height, and had all his brown hair.

"I'm Larry. This is my colleague, Kell." The dude glanced at me. I swear he looked right at the pocket where my gun was hidden. I willed myself not to feel for it.

"Ken," the dude said and then motioned us inside. The door closed, and he got right down to business. "What can I do for you?"

All three of us remained standing in the middle of the room. He wanted us in and out. I was up for that.

The room, a combination kitchen/living and dining area, was set up like an office. There was a desk and mesh chair, a plaid sofa, a smoked glass coffee table, and two red upholstered chairs.

It was tidy and cheap.

No one else appeared to be in the unit. There were two doors on either side of the room which I assumed were bathrooms and or bedrooms. I also guessed the unit was a rental, mainly used for drug deals and other criminal activities.

"We're offering you a business proposition," Larry said. I was glad he did the talking. "Hear us out. If you don't want any part of it, just say it. It'll be like our chat never happened."

Blue Eyes didn't change expression. He was a cool customer or good actor. He glanced at me again. I lifted my chin, hoping I appeared tougher than I was. He looked back at Larry.

"Fifty thousand if you tell us who hired you for the Martinez project," Larry said.

Blue Eyes tapped his right foot a couple times. I kept my eyes on his face, but was aware of his hands.

"That's a lot of money for a name," he said.

"Our client is willing to pay it," Larry said. "Again, no hard feelings if you're not interested."

"You're not the client?" he asked.

Larry shook his head. "Middle man."

Blue Eyes looked at me like he knew what I was about. "Do I have to make a decision now?" he asked me.

Larry answered. "How much time do you need?"

Enough time to call the other guy and see if he'll meet or beat our offer. What would I do? Personally, I don't think I'd contact the other guy because the whole thing would start to get complicated. Scary. A scenario with lots of bodies. Fifty thousand was enough to make me want to simplify everything. Give up a client's name for fifty thousand? Easy work. Why not? What if I was in love with the client? I'd blow the fuckers away but probably not in this makeshift office.

"I'll let you know within twenty-four hours," he said.

I wasn't happy. I wanted it done.

"If we don't hear from you," Larry said, "we'll know you're

not interested. We won't bother you again."

We got to the door when Blue Eyes said, "Wait a minute. I don't need any time."

I was primed, ready to pull my gun.

"This was a two-parter," he said. "I'll give you the name of who paid for the hit on Martinez. You give me fifty thousand."

We sat down on the plaid sofa. The dude eased into one of the red chairs. Larry set the briefcase on the glass coffee table, opened it, and showed Blue Eyes the baggies inside. He then removed the bagged cash, one by one, and set them on the table.

Blue Eyes gave us the name and told us a few other interesting things. That was that. We shook hands, and Larry and I headed for the door.

"Hey," Blue Eyes said to me.

Larry stepped outside to give us a few feet of space, but kept a wary eye on me, which I appreciated.

"Can I get your number?" the hit man asked.

What the fuck? "I'm seeing someone," I said. These were the first words I'd said during the entire meeting.

Blue Eyes chuckled. "So am I," he said. "It's not that. I want to talk to you about something."

Larry stayed quiet, figuring it was my deal, that I could take care of myself.

"We should talk," the hit man said.

"Contact me through this guy," I said, pointing at Larry.

"Sure, sure," he said.

Larry laughed like a maniac when we got in the car. "What the fuck?" he said. "Was he coming on to you? I can't take you anywhere."

"What was his deal?" I laughed too, but didn't find it as funny as Larry. It rattled me.

Larry quickly lost the grin because now we had to tell Rosa what we'd found out.

"He wasn't in love," he said.

"No," I said. "He definitely hadn't fallen in love. Something's not right, Larry."

He glanced at me. "You're right. There's a hink in the dink."

"Two-parter?" I asked. "What do you think that means?"

"You tell me. Have you ever used that term?"

"Never. I have no context for it."

"If someone told you something was a two-parter, what would you think?"

I shrugged. "Two hits, I guess."

"Uh-huh. Maybe two people are already dead. Maybe someone's next."

"Maybe he meant the hit and then the frame."

"Maybe," Larry said, rubbing his face. "Another thing. Why did he tell us it was a two-parter? He intentionally put it out there, but I don't know why."

We drove back to Rosa's. Both of us were quiet, thinking, doing math problems in our heads, only they weren't real math problems.

TWENTY-TWO

"You get a name?"

Rosa was waiting for us in the living room. She rubbed her hands like she was cold. Her face was flushed, and she was breathing hard.

Valerie, who'd been in the kitchen, wandered into the living room. She wiped her hands with a blue towel and had a puzzled look on her beautiful face. "What's going on?"

No one said anything for a long time.

"Rosa?" Valerie asked.

"Can I tell her?" Rosa asked Larry.

"Kell and I met with the hit man," Larry said to Valerie.

Larry and I exchanged glances, and then he looked at Rosa. "I need to talk to you alone," he told her.

"Why?" Valerie asked. Her voice was raised, shrill. She stepped forward. "Absolutely not. Say it in front of me. Rosa, make him." Valerie was coming undone.

Rosa put a hand on her arm. "Tell me in front of Valerie. It's cool. He took the money?"

Larry nodded.

"Give me the name of who hired him," Rosa said.

"Buddy Bach," Larry said.

Valerie's hand went to her mouth. Rosa remained stoic. She was thinking, going through everything in her head. Doing her own math problems.

Valerie sat down hard on the sofa. Rosa sat down too, but eased her way down like a woman on an unfamiliar toilet. Larry and I remained quiet, letting Rosa do the computations in her head.

"Okay," Rosa finally said. "I don't understand how Kell and the hit man ended up in the same place at almost the same time. It's too much of a coincidence. Isn't it, Larry?"

"The coincidence," Larry said, "as near as I can figure, is that you and Buddy are both murderous bastards. I say that with all due respect, Rosa."

Rosa nodded, acknowledging Larry's semi-apology. "What would have happened if Kell hadn't taken the phone call?" She asked it out loud, but was answering it in her head.

"Confusion," Larry said. "Unless it was love at first sight." He shot me a glance. "I'm guessing the best hit man would have won."

Rosa shook her head and put her hands to her face. "I don't understand why," she said. "He'd retire. Turn over everything to Valerie and me. He'd get a commission for the rest of his life. A healthy one. It was generous. He'd retire in style. Never have to worry about money. More than enough."

"He wanted more," Larry said.

"Maybe someone set him up," Rosa said.

She'd taken only one step on the clue bus. It was sad and endearing at the same time. I doubt anyone had ever fooled Rosa so badly.

Valerie remained quiet, her mouth open with bewilderment.

"I don't see it, Rosa," Larry said.

"Why didn't he just kill me?" Rosa asked.

Everything had already gone clickety-clack in my head. Rosa couldn't see it because she was too close. She'd get there, but she was still in denial. No one wants to think someone you trust could betray you so horribly.

"Because he could get Martinez *and* you this way," Larry said. "The original plan was for it to be vice versa. You were the target. Martinez would get framed."

"*She* was the original target?" Valerie asked.

"Buddy apparently got spooked when Kell showed up in Miami," Larry said. "He figured something was up when you brought a security consultant to town to look at the house and office."

I already knew what Rosa would do. When she figured it out, yeah, she'd look at me.

"I still don't understand why," Rosa said.

"It's what it always is, Rosa," Larry said.

"Money, honey," I said.

"I was the original target," she said and looked at Valerie.

"Did you tell him that Kell was your bodyguard?" Larry asked.

"No," Rosa said.

"He thought she was," he said.

"He asked questions about security at the office and here," I said to Larry, but it was for her benefit.

Valerie leaned back and carefully folded the towel she'd been clutching.

"I don't get it," Rosa said. "The company was doing great."

"*Your* company was doing great," Larry said. "His wasn't. I studied the financial records. You bought at the low end. He bought at the peak. You had to have seen that."

"I did see it," she said, like she only now realized it. "I didn't think of it that way, though. I didn't see it as his company and our company. Because we were to inherit everything."

"Valerie was," Larry said.

"Same thing," Valerie said.

"Not if Rosa's dead," he said to her, and then looked back at Rosa. "When he bought, everything was overpriced. Everywhere. Not just Miami. You're in the black. He's in the red. He wanted what you had."

A sudden realization hit Rosa. "A few months ago," she said, "I looked at the books. I saw a transfer from our company into his. About a quarter million. I went to him when I couldn't figure it out." She shook her head. "He was convincing. He couldn't understand it either. He finally told me it must have been his mistake. He was embarrassed. Losing a step, he said. Then it happened again a few weeks ago. It was even more money. This time it was better hidden. Probably only someone with an accounting background would have noticed it. I took it to him. He wept and told me he'd retire. Making too many mistakes, he said. Of course, I talked him out of it. I can't tell you how convincing he was. He was shocked at the mistakes." She made a moaning sound.

"Another thing—" Larry paused.

Okay, I'd been dead wrong about the marble guy, but my instincts were back where they were supposed to be. I knew what'd he say. I was curious how he'd say it.

"He wasn't happy about Valerie staying here," Larry said. "With you."

Rosa shook her head. "They don't have a problem with us. The only thing they care about is that we be discreet in public. We are."

"It wasn't that," he said. "He has this idea—"

Larry was reluctant to continue.

"Go on," Rosa said.

"What did he think?" Valerie asked.

Larry looked at her. "He thought Rosa was pimping you."

Valerie put her head in her hands. Rosa paled.

Rosa had met Valerie in Vegas when Valerie was a working girl. I didn't know much more than that and never asked because, frankly, it wasn't any of my damn business. Rosa told me what she wanted to tell me. Some things are fucking private.

"He apparently hired a private detective—"

"It's not true," Rosa said. "Kell, tell him." It was important to her that Larry believe this.

I nodded. It was true as far as I knew.

"I was an escort in Vegas when I met her," Valerie said. She shook her head. "I can't believe he found out about that. That is so embarrassing." She looked at Rosa. "He must have assumed that's how we met."

There was an uncomfortable silence. Larry and I wanted to know more but had enough manners not to ask.

Rosa looked at me. "Look, Kell," she said, "you know I met Valerie in Vegas. I told you that."

I nodded.

"I told you how I met her," Rosa said.

"You told me she was a working girl," I said. "You didn't give details."

"It's not that big a deal. It's not like I hired her. We were both in a casino. She was escorting. I was alone, playing slot machines. She saw me. I saw her. We hooked up."

"Were you working for someone?" Larry asked Valerie.

"Yes," she said. "I quit right after I met Rosa. We stayed in Vegas about a week after that. Then I came back here. Until I went to Atlanta."

Here's where it got sticky. Rosa went back to Chicago and came up with a plan to get out of the business. Part of the plan involved sending me to Atlanta where I'd kill a guy named Hank Kingsley, and then get offed by Valerie. It wasn't a good plan. Rosa admitted it later. The only part that succeeded was poor Hank got killed.

Rosa and Valerie were embarrassed about the incident. Still, this seemed as good a time as any for me to find out more.

"How was Hank Kingsley involved?" I asked.

"It got so complicated," Rosa said. She glanced at Valerie. "She doesn't know this."

Valerie's face tightened. She gave Rosa a 'What now?' look.

"The guy Valerie worked for didn't want to let her go," Rosa said.

"Nink," Valerie said.

"Nink," Rosa said. "He wanted something in return, so Hank Kingsley had to go. I think it had to do with a woman, but I never knew for sure. So, Kell, you got sent to Atlanta."

"Why didn't you tell me?" Valerie asked.

"I was afraid you'd stay in Vegas if you knew he was making trouble," Rosa said. "I also wanted you to be able to say you didn't know anything if Kell or anyone asked you."

There was a long silence while we processed.

"How long had you been working in Vegas?" Larry asked Valerie.

"A year or so," she said. "It was something I fell into."

Larry raised his hands as if to say he wasn't judging.

"I was stupid," Valerie explained. "Immature. I thought I was smarter than everyone else. Uncle Buddy wanted me to join the business. I thought it made more sense to work only a few hours a week and make thousands. Look, guys get stupid around me. I could get them to give me money and things. It seemed a natural thing. I'd done plays in high school. It was just more acting. I could make lots of money. I'm mortified that Uncle Buddy and Aunt Marie found out about it."

Larry cleared his throat. There was more. "Your Uncle Buddy was under the impression that Rosa was pimping you here."

Rosa and Valerie tried to make sense of what he said.

"For the company," he said. "To make deals."

Valerie reddened. Rosa closed her eyes and shook her head. "Absolutely not," she said. "It's not even close to true."

"Apparently it's a rumor that's been going around," Larry said.

"Never," Rosa said. "We both tried to go legit after—" Our eyes met. "Uncle Buddy couldn't possibly have known about me. What Ironclad was."

"I think you're right about that because if he did he probably wouldn't have done what he did," Larry said.

"Who told you this stuff?" Rosa asked.

"I have a variety of sources," Larry said.

"So everyone in Miami thinks I'm a hooker?" Valerie asked.

"I wouldn't say everyone believes it, but that's the gossip," he said.

"Did he fake the heart attack?" Rosa asked.

"I don't know," Larry said. "I can't get his medical records, and even if I could—"

"He might have," Rosa said. "To give Valerie an alibi."

"How did he know you wouldn't go with Valerie to the hospital?" Larry asked.

"I guess I never have." Rosa looked at Valerie. "Have I?"

"You've got that thing about hospitals," Valerie said.

"You've got a thing about hospitals?" I asked. This was news to me.

"I don't like them," Rosa said.

"I didn't know that," I said.

"I'm an enigma," she said.

"Rosa, both your parents worked in hospitals," I said.

She shrugged. "I've never visited him in the hospital."

"What if I were in the hospital?" I asked.

"Sweetie, if you were in the hospital, I'd come," Rosa said.

That was a fucking relief.

Rosa looked at Larry. "He got people to say they saw me in Martinez's neighborhood," she said. "I guess he paid them."

"He paid them half," Larry said.

Rosa thought for a moment and then nodded. "So when they testify, they get the second half. How did he pay them?"

"It's a guess," Larry said. "Laundered through his attorney. All the witnesses have some connection to Ray Regina."

Larry got someone to give up the names of three witnesses. It had to be someone in law enforcement. This was a tricky area.

Smacked of witness tampering and worse. My suspicion was he found a dirty cop. Everyone has a price.

Rosa closed her eyes. When she opened them, she was driving the clue bus. "Ray. That's why he gave me bad advice. It was a good setup."

The room remained tense for several moments. Rosa looked at Valerie for a long time. Finally, Rosa reluctantly nodded. Valerie closed her eyes and nodded back. The towel went up to her face.

"Larry, I need to talk to Kell and Valerie for a few minutes," Rosa calmly said.

Larry stood. "If you don't mind, Rosa, I'd like a word with Kell."

Rosa's expression said she did mind but motioned him to go ahead. Her demeanor had totally changed. This was the Rosa I was used to dealing with.

"Kell," he said.

I followed him to his room. He closed the door.

"I'm not telling you what to do," Larry said, "but I have strong reservations about you working with Rosa on this."

"I understand."

"I'm leaving, Kell. I'll be out of town. Do you understand what I'm saying?" Larry didn't want anything to do with what was coming next.

"Yes."

"She'll try to talk you into it." He meant Rosa. "You don't have to. You can say no."

"There's no one else."

"She can hire someone else."

I shook my head. He shook his.

"I'm worried," Larry said. "Look, I'm fond of Rosa. I'd do just about anything for her. But not this. There's a bad voodoo feeling about it. You're walking into something."

"You think Uncle Buddy is a crack shot?"

"I was thinking Aunt Marie. Listen, Kell, it's got a bad vibe to it. On so many levels."

"She doesn't have anyone else."

"I'll try to find someone."

It was cute that he was protective of me. I lightly kissed him on the cheek. "Larry, I'm the only person she can trust. We can't bring someone else into it now. A stranger? No way."

"Let me get out of town before it happens then."

Who can blame him? He didn't want blood on his hands. "I'll take you to the airport," I said.

He sighed. He thought he'd changed my mind. It was wishful thinking.

"Have you ever told her no on anything?" he asked.

"Larry, I don't have a choice."

"But you do. That's what I want you to see. It might be the first time, but say no to her. Let her find someone else or let the whole thing go. Sylvia is a great lawyer. Let her do her job."

I didn't say anything. He realized he couldn't talk me out of it, and wasn't happy about it.

"If anything happens to you," he said, "and Gin finds out I had anything to do with it, I won't get a fair hearing. She'll leave my lying ass."

I shook my head. "Don't worry about it," I said. "For one thing, she'll never find out. For another, she's off me right now. The last time I talked to her, let's just say I didn't find her sympathetic to my cause." I talked in a hard tone. "She's totally on Gretchen's side. She wouldn't care if something happened to me."

"You're wrong about that."

"Larry, she was cold to me. Stone cold. I was crying. She cut me off."

"She may have acted that way with you on the phone, but believe me she's not cold about you."

"Whatever. We may be sisters, but she doesn't feel sisterly

toward me. Even you have to admit she's more like a sister to Gretchen."

He couldn't argue with that. "All I'm saying is that she worries about you. She doesn't understand you, but—"

"She liked me better when I was her student. As a sister—" I shook my head. "I'm too much trouble."

"If something happens to you, and she thinks I'm responsible, she'll leave me and never have anything to do with me again."

"Yeah. We'll see."

"I don't want to see. Kell, please think about it. If you keep doing things like this, eventually you'll get caught or worse. Even you admitted you've lost a step."

I glared at him.

"I'm worried about you," he said, tapping my chest with his finger.

"I'll-be-fine."

For a moment, I thought he'd change his mind and stay. Instead, he shook his head. "I'm leaving. Please be careful. If something doesn't feel right—"

"I'll be fine," I repeated. I gave him a short, terse hug and pushed him away. "Go pack. We'll get you out of here since you can't handle it."

I immediately felt guilty for being a bitch. "Sorry I got you into this, Larry. I know it's not your thing."

He waved me off and started packing.

TWENTY-THREE

I rejoined Rosa and Valerie in the living room. Rosa was calm, acting like it was any other job. She and Valerie had talked while I was with Larry because things were already worked out.

"Kell, tomorrow afternoon Valerie will get over there around one p.m.," Rosa said. "She'll have tea and cookies with them. While she makes the tea, she's putting antihistamine powder in their cups. Around three, they'll get sleepy. She'll suggest they nap. She'll walk them back to their room and put them in bed. She's done this before, so it won't arouse suspicion. You'll be waiting in the back yard. Take gloves." She paused. "That landscaping thing we talked about?"

I nodded.

"Use it this time," Rosa said.

Some time ago, I'd mentioned to Rosa how a hit man could pose as a landscaper. It occurred to me one day when I observed my gardener, Nicole Westlake, working around my neighborhood. It was like she was invisible. She had access to everyone's yards No one questioned her. Rosa had apparently stored the information in her computer-like brain.

"There is no video camera," Rosa continued. "No dogs. No bodyguards. She'll leave the back door unlocked. The code to turn off the alarm is three-two-one. Valerie will leave their house about three-fifteen. Before she leaves, she'll set a loaded handgun on the bedroom dresser near the door. She'll pass you on the way out, so you'll know for sure. Put on the gloves. Go inside the house." Rosa motioned with her left hand. "You walk through the kitchen into the living room. The hall is to your right." She motioned with her right hand. "When you get to the hallway, you turn left and go forward to the bedroom at the end of the hall. The dresser is on your immediate left. She'll put the gun on the corner nearest you along with a handkerchief." She paused. "You will take care of both."

She looked at me to make sure I got it. I nodded.

"This is a murder-suicide," Rosa said. "Put the handkerchief in your pocket and get out."

"Is he right-handed?" I asked.

Rosa thought for a moment. "Yes."

Valerie cooked Cuban again. No one said much during dinner.

After the dishes were cleared, we congregated on the patio. The intense heat had cooled due to a sudden, brief rainstorm, and there was a light breeze. If it was like this all the time, everyone would live in Miami.

Larry started a conversation about Cuba. Valerie explained how she'd twice violated the travel embargo to visit Cuba with her mother. Larry was fascinated, or at least pretended to be.

Rosa motioned to me. "I need to talk to you for a minute," she whispered.

Valerie briefly stopped talking to Larry when she saw us go off together but quickly returned to the conversation when Rosa indicated she'd be back in a minute.

Once inside, we sat in chairs across from each other at the island. Rosa got down to business.

"Tell me about the hit man," Rosa said.

"What do you want to know?"

"Describe him."

"About six feet tall. Brown hair. Cut short. Got all his hair. Blue eyes. Slight build. Why?"

"I think I know him."

This chilled me.

"How?"

"I saw a guy at the office a few times," Rosa said. "He wore a uniform and carried boxes like he was a delivery guy. But he wasn't postal service, UPS, or Fed Ex."

"Striking blue eyes."

She nodded. "You and Larry said I was the original target."

"You think he was scoping you?"

"I think it's the same guy. Something didn't feel right with him. He never came to our office, but I saw him a few times." She paused. "I'd like to think you'd be better about it."

"I'd like to think so too. When's the last time you saw him?"

"I'm not sure." Rosa shivered. "I came close, didn't I?"

"When's the last time you saw him?" I asked again. "This is important, Rosa. Since I've been here?"

She nodded. "I don't remember the day. Maybe a week ago. Definitely before you met with him."

"I wonder when he changed his mind and went with Martinez instead?" When I said 'he,' I meant Uncle Buddy. I'd taken Rosa's lead and decided not to say his name.

"Obviously after that."

"Uh-huh."

Rosa settled back into her chair, but then immediately stood. "I need to turn down the air. Don't you think it's too cold in here?"

Rosa and Valerie left for work the next morning while I dropped off Larry at the airport. I didn't get out of the car with him.

"Take care of yourself," he said, without looking at me, and was gone.

His disapproval bothered me more than I wanted to admit.

I had several hours to kill, so I drove around, stopping at different beaches. I bought a cheese sub at a sandwich place near Haulover, the nude beach. There wasn't much to see. People who want to run around naked are never the people you want to see naked.

I drove to the targets' neighborhood, parked down the street, and walked to their house. Valerie made a thrift store run the night before, so I was dressed as a landscaper with olive cargos, a straw hat, and a khaki t-shirt. I had pruners jammed in a holster clipped on my belt. The gloves and gun were in my utility pockets.

I strolled to the back yard and reached for the pruners when my phone vibrated. Yeah. I shouldn't have brought it with me. Gretchen's timing was fucking unbelievable. I'd turned off the phone the previous night and powered it back on in the morning. She'd already left a couple messages that I hadn't listened to. Gretchen left another message. I shut off the fucking phone.

I pulled out my pruners and snipped at branches near the back door. I had no idea what I was doing, but mimicked what I'd seen Nicole do.

As I waited, I had time to think. This was grim business. I wondered what it would do to Rosa's relationship with Valerie. I thought I had issues with Gretchen, but killing family members? That was fucked up.

Valerie was inside saying her goodbyes, only Aunt Marie and Uncle Buddy didn't know. Rosa and Valerie agreed that it had to be both. They had no idea how much Aunt Marie knew, but the poor woman was in bad health and would have a hard time without Buddy. To be honest, if I was Aunt Marie I would have asked someone to kill me a long time ago.

I understood why Rosa made Valerie part of this plan. Her

participation wasn't necessary. There were any number of ways I could get inside the house. Rosa intentionally included Valerie, so she'd be tied to it. It's not that she didn't trust Valerie, but this was extra insurance if Valerie ever decided she didn't like what went down.

It got be three-fifteen. I was sweating. My hand hurt from cutting. How could Nicole stand this? Pruning was tedious and a pain in the ass.

I wanted to get it over with. Some hits are more unpleasant than others. This one was fucking unpleasant. I prefer my hits to be impersonal. This was too personal. I'd eaten with these people. Helped diaper Aunt Marie.

Now it was three-thirty. The bushes weren't looking great, and Valerie still hadn't come out of the fucking house. I went through all my options. If it got much later, I'd leave. We'd try another time.

Just when I decided to ditch the plan, Valerie came out the back door and brushed past me, arms tightly crossed, without saying a word. She was crying. That didn't make me want to go inside. Still, I slipped the pruners in the holster and opened the door. Once inside, I typed the security code into the panel next to the back door.

Everything was quiet. Valerie had betrayed me in the past. I couldn't help wondering if it might happen again.

I took a step and listened. Nothing.

The exterior of the house hadn't been much, just a white brick ranch, but the interior was money. Expensive-looking oil paintings were on the walls. The place was loaded with heavy antique furniture and brocaded drapery. Thick oriental rugs covered the floors. Beautiful bookcases showcased books that appeared to have been bought for their matching bindings.

A family photo grouping sat on top of the grand piano in the living room, including a photo of Valerie and Rosa and what was probably Valerie's high school graduation photo. And Buddy and

Marie's wedding picture was there too. It messed with me.

I found the hallway to the bedroom and headed down it. I won't lie to you. I was nervous about walking through that doorway, wondering if Uncle Buddy and Aunt Marie were sitting up in bed with automatics pointed at me. Or maybe they weren't there. I didn't want any fucking surprises.

There weren't any. Uncle Buddy and Aunt Marie were asleep, on the bed in their clothing, covers pulled up to their necks. They faced each other. I watched the covers slowly rise and fall.

I picked up the handgun with the handkerchief. This was the weak link. I like to work with a silencer. I also like to work with a familiar gun. I had neither luxury today.

If the gun jammed, I was fucked. I'd already decided if it happened I'd kill both with my own gun. The murder-suicide would be gone, and we'd be in a bad situation.

I crept up to the bed, disengaged the safety, and shot Aunt Marie in the forehead. I did her first because I didn't want to risk even a second of her feeling fear. Immediately, just after he opened his eyes, I shot Uncle Buddy in the temple, put the gun in his right hand, put my hand around his, and squeezed the trigger, shooting Aunt Marie in the heart. I cringed, and I'm not a cringer. I arranged the scene and pocketed the handkerchief. Then I got the fuck out of there.

TWENTY-FOUR

I finally checked my voicemails after I sank into my car. Gretchen had left three. The first was from last night. It was civil. The second, left this morning, was of the, "I'm not sure why you haven't called back yet" variety.

The third, the one I got just before the hit, was angry. "You're not returning my phone calls. Fine. Just let me know you're okay, and I'll leave you alone. Just fucking call me back, Kell."

I turned off the phone and drove aimlessly around Miami. Rosa and Valerie were at work, and the house was empty.

I ended up in the Sands Motel parking lot not far from the ocean. It advertised that its rate was $29.99 a night which looked expensive from what I saw. It was an L-shaped white frame building with faded turquoise doors and dirty windows. The ocean was two blocks away.

I thought about walking to the beach, maybe picking up a girl. Not sex. Just making out.

I thought about it awhile but ended up doing nothing. Fuck it.

I drove back to Rosa's and sat around until they came back. I nodded to Rosa when she came in. She took a deep breath and let it out slowly. Valerie didn't look at me when she returned.

Rosa ordered in food from a deli. Sandwiches, chips, and

Cokes. That's what we ate for dinner. No one had an appetite. We didn't talk much.

Rosa had decided that rather than have Valerie 'discover' the bodies, we'd leave it to the cleaning woman to find them. She was scheduled to clean the following morning.

"I need to take a shower," I said, after we ate.

"Do you mind if we come in too?" Rosa asked.

"No. I don't mind."

It led to what you'd expect. It got me thinking about renovating my house's bathroom with black and white marble slate and two shower heads. I might even spring for the cedar sauna.

Valerie wasn't into it. She's a gamer, though, and we continued in their bedroom. One time, when Valerie got up to get water, Rosa straddled me, tongue kissed me hard for a long time, and then pulled back. "I really do love you, Kell."

"I love you too, Rosa."

That's all the time we had before Valerie returned. I gave Valerie extra attention because she was hurting.

She had a hard time coming. Unusual for her. When she finally came, it was a good one.

Hours later, I woke up and realized Valerie was gone from the bed. Rosa was lying on her side, asleep. I carefully got out of bed and left the room.

I figured I knew what Valerie was doing. I was right. I found her sitting outside by the pool, wrapped in a blanket and crying. She let me hold her.

There was nothing I could say. The two people she loved more than anyone else in the world, except for Rosa, were dead. It was a huge loss, and knowing she'd betrayed them made it worse. You could argue for a week, but it wouldn't make any difference. This was a line from Larry's beloved TV show, *Dragnet*, and it was the fucking truth.

I was naked, and my flesh turned to goose bumps. Valerie must have realized because she opened up the blanket and let me in.

"You can talk if you want," I said.

"I don't want to," she said. But then she started talking. "I know they loved me. Everything he did, he did for me. That makes me so sad. It would have been better if we'd never come to Miami." Every sentence was like a separate, mismatched bead. "I told them I loved them every time I saw them. They were both so sick at the end. I don't ever want to live that long. They were so much a part of my routine. He was wrong about Rosa."

She wiped her wet face with her hand. "I don't know how you do what you do."

I couldn't think of an answer, so I remained quiet.

"They weren't scared, were they?" she asked.

"They never knew I was there."

She heaved an uneasy sigh and cried again. I held her close and kissed her forehead. She pulled herself together after a few minutes.

"Tell me about your girlfriend," she said. "What's she like?"

"Normal."

She laughed, partly to have a release. "How much have you told her?"

"Not much. I get the feeling she doesn't want to know. And, yeah, I'm afraid she'll dump me for good if she knows everything."

"Rosa and I tell each other everything. Pretty much. She told me she fantasizes about you."

I found this interesting. "Did it hurt your feelings?"

"No. You'd think it would, but it didn't. You two have a strong bond. It's a strange one though. I told her I fantasized about you too."

"Is that what led her to ask me to come to Miami?"

"I know you think it did, but that's not it. She was concerned about you. She said you get into dark moods and don't take care of yourself. What we did to you in Atlanta was about the worst thing you can do to another person. It's hard to understand it now. She thought it was the best thing. She thought of you as almost feral. I don't think I could have forgiven either of us. There's a part of me that still thinks you'll turn on us." She burrowed in deeper to me. "Do you fantasize about us?"

"Yes."

"Did you tell your girlfriend?"

"No."

"Will you tell her about—?"

"No," I said.

"You don't know what—"

"I won't tell her anything."

She kissed me. It was a long kiss that drugged me.

"Thanks," she said, when we stopped. "You're a good kid."

It's a funny statement because she's younger than me, but I know what she meant.

"Do you ever wonder if this is really happening?" Valerie asked.

I didn't know where she was going, so I stayed quiet.

"I get crazy thoughts sometimes," Valerie said. "None of this makes sense. Let's say that when we were in Georgia you hurt me. Put me in a coma."

My teeth clicked.

"And," Valerie continued, "this is something I've created in my coma. Or maybe I'm in your coma."

"You mean, you didn't graze me. You—"

"Yes."

"Shot me in the head, and I'm in a coma. Makes as much sense as anything else."

"I'll tell Rosa we were out at the pool and made out," she said.

"I figured."

"Let's get our money's worth."

We kissed a while longer and then went back inside and crawled in next to Rosa.

"You know, kid," Rosa said to me the next day, "if you hadn't come to Miami I'd be dead or in prison. You and your boyfriend saved me."

I smiled at the mention of Larry.

"You're quite a team," she said.

Valerie was with her family making arrangements, meeting with attorneys, and all the things you have to do when family members die. When Valerie had gotten the call at the office at eleven a.m., Rosa shut everything down, sent Dolores and Dana home, and returned to the house.

"Will you guys be okay?" I asked.

"We've talked about visiting Greece until everything blows over. Maybe stay a while." She shook her head. "I can't believe I got conned. *Me*. It's karma." She shuddered. "This Miami real estate business is cut-throat. We're getting out."

"Going back to the stability of contract killing."

"Haven't decided."

I wondered. "I'm not doing it again, Rosa."

"I understand."

I hoped she did. Guilt coated me like chocolate on a Milky Way bar. It was an unfamiliar feeling after a hit, and I never wanted to feel it again.

"What will you do about Gretchen?" she asked.

"Larry thinks I should drive to California. I don't think it's a good idea. He thinks it'll mean something to her. I'm afraid it'll seem overly aggressive. What do you think?"

"I don't know her well enough to say, Kell. She asked you to give her space."

"That's exactly what I told him."

"But she might think it romantic that you drove clear across the country to see her." Rosa shrugged. "Who knows about women?"

"You do all right."

"Are you angry?" she asked.

I had a lot of emotions, but anger wasn't one of them. "No."

"You can stay if you want."

"It's crossed my mind. I want to give it another shot with Gretchen. This—" I motioned to her. "This would be easy."

"Kell, she'll come back to you. She won't be able to forget you. Trust me."

"I don't know about that, Rosa."

"I do. When she comes back, you 'Yes, ma'am' her for a good long time. If that's what you want. Valerie told me about you guys making out by the pool."

An apology would be disingenuous.

"She said you comforted her," Rosa said. "One thing led to another."

Rosa gave me a chance to respond. I didn't take it.

"I'm not mad," she said. "Would you have told me?"

"She said she'd tell you. Gretchen's called a few times. I haven't returned her calls."

Rosa winced. "Ooh," she said, shaking her head.

"I'm not in the right frame of mind," I said.

Rosa frowned. "Women hate it when their calls aren't returned. You need to call."

"I don't have the right words," I said.

"Find them. Now."

I strolled back to my room and punched Gretchen's number. While I waited for the connection, I stretched out on the bed. Gretchen picked up on the first ring and was loaded for bear.

"Why haven't you called me back?" she shouted.

"I'm sorry."

"Honestly, Kell, I don't get you at all."

Everything hit me. If I hadn't cheated on Gretchen, I

wouldn't be in Miami. If I wasn't in Miami, Uncle Buddy and Aunt Marie would be alive. Still, Rosa was right. If I wasn't here, she'd probably be dead.

"Say something," she said.

"Maybe we're too different."

"*That's* what you've decided," she said.

I wanted to tell her that I was sorry I'd brought her into my life, that I'd been selfish. I also wanted to tell her to hook up with a respectable woman and forget about me. On the verge of tears, I breathed uneasily a few times.

"You're not coping well, are you?" she asked.

She imagined I was at the Stone Mountain house, maybe curled up in our unmade bed. She'd kick my ass if she knew I was in Miami.

"You get distant from me when we aren't getting along," she said. "It drives me nuts when you don't return my calls."

I struggled to get hold of myself. Gretchen kept saying things about how I'd be fine, maybe I should go to the 'p-a-r-k' because that always seemed to do me good. She was cheering me up, for God's sake.

"Will you agree to couples counseling?" Gretchen asked.

"I'll do anything," I heard myself say. "Couples counseling. Anything." What the *fuck*? Who'd taken over my fucking mouth?

"You will?"

"Absolutely." Absolutely sure I didn't want to go to couples counseling, but I wanted Gretchen back. My feeling was once I got her back, she'd forget about the stupid counseling.

While Gretchen thought about my response, Rosa stalked in the room, phone pressed against her chest. The expression on her face jolted my midsection.

"We need to talk face to face," Gretchen said.

Rosa stiffly held the phone out to me. "You need to take this," she said in a low voice.

I sat up. "Gretchen, I have to take care of something. I'll call back."

She didn't say anything, and I hung up.

TWENTY-FIVE

"It's for you," Rosa said. "Ken."

I took the phone. "Yeah."

"We met the other day. You were with a big guy."

"Yeah, I remember," I said.

Rosa hovered. "Who is he?" she whispered.

"What do you want?" I asked. I pantomimed to Rosa that I needed to write something.

Rosa hurriedly handed me a pad of paper and pen from the nightstand's drawer. I quickly wrote "HIT MAN," flashed it to her, and quickly and decisively crossed it out, completing blacking out every letter.

Rosa grabbed the notepad and pen and wrote, "WHY?????"

I shrugged my shoulders.

"I saw you," he said. "That day. I saw you sitting on the bench at the plaza. You were on the phone having an argument."

"You were already there?" I was totally off-balance with the conversation.

"Yes," he said. "I was looking out the second floor window. You were on your way to Martinez's, weren't you?"

I didn't answer.

He chuckled. "Amazing, isn't it? I kept watching you. After you hung up, I went out the back. I assume you went inside the building."

I didn't say anything.

"Remarkable coincidence, don't you think?"

I was disoriented, like I was in a funhouse. Maybe the conversation was being recorded. Maybe Ken was a cop. I got hit with a painful wave. Maybe Larry and I had been played.

"Hey, I'm not trying to freak you out," he said. "We've got a lot in common. That's why I wanted us to talk. Don't you think there's a connection between us?"

The only connection, I wanted to tell Ken, is that we're both murderous bastards.

Maybe Ken and I had a connection. Maybe we didn't. Maybe Ken was playing me, though I couldn't figure out why or what he wanted.

"You were arguing with your girlfriend, weren't you?" he asked. "Are you still there?"

"Yeah."

"Right before I did it, I had an argument with my partner. We've got these weird parallel lives. I'm not sure what it means. I felt a kindred spirit. That's why I wanted to talk to you."

"So talk."

"What does he want?" Rosa mouthed.

I shook my head. Damned if I knew.

"Do you remember when I told you this was a two-parter?" he asked.

"Yeah."

"Do you know what I meant?"

I didn't answer.

"Does that mean no?" he asked. "Are you there?"

"Yeah."

"I wanted to give you a head's up that you triggered the second part."

Ken hung up. I shakily handed the phone back to Rosa.

"What did he say when you answered?" I asked.

"He asked for Kell. I asked who was calling. He said Ken.

Then he said something like, 'She'll want to take this call. It's about Buddy Bach.'"

I told Rosa most of what he'd said. She insisted that I call Larry.

"No," I said.

She looked at me like I was crazy.

"He can't come back to Miami," I said. "There's nothing he can do."

"Call Sylvia," Rosa ordered.

"And say what?"

"That someone's made a threat."

"It's a can of worms, Rosa." I tried to be gentle, but was freaked out and barely in control.

"Do you think he's on your side? Truly giving you a head's up?"

"My gut tells me no."

"You think he's poking at you?"

"That's my feeling."

I went back to my room, got my gun, and then paced around the house, holding the gun, looking out windows, sorting things out.

Rosa shadowed me, arms crossed, wanting to do something, but not knowing what she should do.

"Stay away from the windows," I cautioned, motioning her away.

"Tell me what you're thinking."

"Give me a minute."

"What do you think he meant about triggering the second part?"

Her voice irritated me. I struggled to keep my cool.

"You think what happened to Uncle Buddy was a trigger?"

I was close to slapping my hand over her mouth to keep her quiet. Rosa realized I wasn't chatty, sighed, and dropped on the sofa.

My first thought was to drive back to the office where I'd met Ken. Like most first thoughts, it was a stupid one. For one thing, he likely wouldn't be there. For another, if he was, I'd walk into an ambush.

It unnerved me what he'd said about us being connected. Maybe he knew how I thought and made decisions too. He'd fucked with me good.

Piece by piece, I figured most things out. One thing I couldn't fathom, though, was why he'd given me a head's up. The only answer I could come up was he enjoyed the game. I'll be damned if I, too, didn't feel a certain sick thrill. Gin was right. I had a chip missing. I was scared, but part of me was excited. It was almost pleasurable. He must be like me, I thought. He even fucked with me when I met him at the condo. It was a dangerous, deadly game, but isn't that what being a hit man was all about?

"When's Valerie getting back?" I asked.

"Not sure," Rosa said.

Valerie was the weak link. If we told her about the phone call, it'd be all over her face. She'd act weird around her family. That may come back to haunt us.

"Want me to call her?" Rosa asked.

"No."

Rosa looked at my gun. "You think someone's coming here?"

"You and I will be glued together until this is resolved. I'll stay awake tonight and make sure you're safe. Tomorrow morning we're all going into your office."

"You think I'm the second part?" she asked, fear contorting her features.

"We'll find out tomorrow," I said. There was one person who could tell us for sure.

"You plan on staying awake all night?"

"Absolutely," I said. "Start the coffee."

"We can sleep in shifts."

I rolled my eyes.

"You've got to sleep, Kell," she said.

"Can you handle a gun?"

A car drove down the street. I stood at attention. It passed. I relaxed.

"Tomorrow we'll go in at nine," I said. "Get Dolores and Dana out of the building."

"You think someone's coming to the office? Tell me what you're thinking."

"He might come here," I said. "I don't know, but there's something I have to do at the office tomorrow. I can't and won't leave you here. I'm not letting you out of my sight." I shook my head. "No fucking way."

"The hit man was playing with you. He wasn't doing you a favor."

A car drove up the driveway. I moved across the room and looked out the window blinds.

"Sounds like Valerie's car," Rosa said.

"Yeah."

I stepped away from the window and got into a shooting position, aiming at the front door.

"What are you doing?" Rosa asked. "Kell."

"If he's out there, he might try to come in with her. Get behind the couch, Rosa. Now. Lie flat on your stomach." I talked quickly, and Rosa did as she was told.

Valerie came through the door and swung it shut. She took a couple steps and caught me out of the corner of her eye, pointing the gun at her with both hands.

Valerie reeled away, backpedaling as fast as she could. She saw Rosa on the floor, assumed the worst, and backed hard into the wall. Instinctively, her hands went up to protect her face. I wasn't pointing the gun at her anymore but at the door. The distinction meant little to Valerie.

She sunk to her knees, made the sign of the cross, and

mumbled something that sounded like a prayer.

"Anyone follow you?" I asked.

"The hit man called and made a threat," Rosa said from the floor.

"I don't think so," Valerie said, her voice shaking.

"You didn't notice anything out of the ordinary?" I asked.

"Just this." Valerie pointed at me, unsure.

I lowered my gun. "I was afraid he was behind you." I motioned for Rosa to get up.

"What did he say?" Valerie asked.

"He said I triggered part two," I said.

"You mean by—"

"That's what we think," Rosa said.

"Shouldn't we call the police?" Valerie asked.

No one said anything.

"What did you tell the cops?" I asked.

"I told the detective they were in bad health," Valerie said. "I didn't notice they were particularly despondent."

I nodded. We'd gone over a script with her.

"I told them it was a surprise to me," Valerie said. "The funeral is in two days."

"Maybe that's when he plans on doing it," Rosa said.

"Do what?" Valerie asked.

I held up my hand to silence them. "I'm still not sure about that," I cautioned Rosa. I was damn sure, but didn't want to talk. I wanted to drink coffee and play around with stuff in my head.

I didn't allow either out of my sight the rest of the night. If someone had to pee, we all went together. Rosa and Valerie agreed, even though I was peeing like a boy dog because of two big cups of strong coffee.

"We really think you should sleep a few hours at least," Rosa said. "If nothing else, so you won't be wiped out tomorrow."

"I'll be fine," I said.

"We'll sit right next to you while you sleep. We'll do it in shifts," Valerie said. "If we hear anything, we'll wake you and give you the gun."

I was, I realized, a bit of a control freak. I didn't trust either to stay awake or respond quickly enough. I would have trusted Larry, but not these two.

"No," I said.

Rosa motioned to Valerie to let it go.

After I put them to bed at ten, I sat between them on the mattress with the gun in my hands.

It took a while, but both eventually fell asleep. Meanwhile, I was antsy and kept hearing noises. I wasn't excited anymore. I was exhausted.

Rosa woke at three a.m., sat up, and nudged me. "Let me take over, Kell. Just an hour or two."

I shook my head. Her fingers touched mine and crawled to the gun.

"Sweetie, you know how much I hate guns," she said. "I'm begging you. I promise I'll wake you up in an hour. I won't screw this up."

An hour of sleep was better than no sleep. I reluctantly showed Rosa how to hold the gun and implored her to wake me if she heard anything.

I probably slept a half hour at most because I kept waking up. Finally, she handed the gun back to me and laid back down.

I didn't dare do anything but guard, not wanting to release my hold on the gun for a moment. Normally I would have been bored to death, but I was keyed up. It also gave me the opportunity to work things out in my head.

By the time Rosa and Valerie got up the next morning, I had a good idea what was up.

TWENTY-SIX

"Do you have a gun in the house?" I asked Rosa. I was eating a peanut butter granola bar in the kitchen. I figured she didn't but hoped she did.

"No," she said.

"Valerie?" I asked.

"No," Valerie emphatically said.

"Do you keep one at the office?" I asked.

"No," Rosa said. "Neither does Valerie. We're not gun people, Kell."

"Do you know where I can get a gun?" I asked.

"Uncle Buddy might have another one," Rosa said.

"I think he does," Valerie said.

"I can't go back there," I said. "Anyone else?"

Rosa shook her head. "I can't think of anyone."

"Do you know where people in Miami go to get a gun?" I asked.

"Not here. Chicago, yeah, but not here."

I was stymied. I didn't want to use my own gun and couldn't buy one legally because it'd be traced to me. I went to plan B.

"Do you have a switchblade?" I asked.

Rosa gave me a look.

"Any sharp weapon," I said.

"All we have are cooking knives," Valerie said.

I found the sharpest knife I could find in a kitchen drawer. I'd never killed anyone like this before and wasn't looking forward to it.

"We're taking the Jag today," I told Rosa and Valerie.

I thoroughly checked out the car and garage before ushering them into the vehicle. With Valerie in the driver's seat, I hit the garage door opener and assumed the stance with my gun in case someone was waiting in the driveway.

I'd done driveway hits in the past. It's easy. You just wait for your target to back out of the garage and blast 'em.

Valerie slowly backed out the car. Convinced no one was lurking in the driveway, I got in the back seat, and we drove downtown to the office building.

"Park on the street," I said, refusing to let Valerie enter the parking garage. "It's a great place for a hit." It was. I'd done two in parking garages myself. There were tons of hiding places. If you knew your target's car you were home free.

"We'll get a ticket for sure, Kell," Rosa moaned. "You don't know Miami."

"It's true, Kell," Valerie said. "They give you tickets even if you have time on the meter."

"I'll pay the fucking ticket," I said.

When we walked in the Green Building, I was wearing a black tank top and blue jeans. I looked fucking unprofessional and figured Adam the doorman would give me a look. Adam did stare at me, but it was more of a leer.

My black backpack held my wallet, the gun and knife, a silencer, and gloves. I didn't take out the gun, but kept it close to me. It wasn't the brightest idea in the world to have the gun on the video cameras.

"Remember," I said to Rosa on the elevator, "get Dolores and Dana out."

Fortunately, both women were in the front office when we came in. Dolores shot me a look of disapproval, apparently thinking I was too casual. Dana flashed me a smile. She didn't care how I dressed.

Rosa is a good actor. Valerie was a different story. Still, the fact she'd lost her aunt and uncle were valid reasons for acting like a basket case.

"Because of Buddy and Marie's passing," Rosa said, "we're closing early today. In fact, you two can leave now."

They were surprised, but Rosa was the boss.

"Tomorrow we'll start at the same time?" Dolores asked.

Rosa looked at me. I shook my head. We'd play it by ear, but it was probably best to tell them that tomorrow would be another off day.

"Buddy's funeral," I said.

Dolores was intrigued that I was giving the orders. Dana, not so much. She lost the smile and slumped. She thought I'd played her and taken a job with Rosa and Valerie, the one she'd set her sights on.

Still, both quickly warmed up to the idea that they were free to leave. It was a beautiful morning, still in the seventies. I waited till they were on the elevator, and then locked the glass door to the suite and pulled out my gun.

I led Rosa and Valerie down the hall to Rosa's office and quickly checked it out. I also thoroughly examined her dark walk-in closet. Inside were copy paper, printer cartridges, and boxes of pens, neatly organized on shelves.

I had to make a quick decision. I could take Rosa and Valerie with me or lock them in the closet. Neither was a great option. I thought about letting them choose, then discarded that stupid idea.

I opened the closet again. "Ladies," I said, motioning them to walk in.

They hesitated.

"Kell, there's no light," Rosa complained.

"There's something I have to do," I said. "Hopefully, it won't take long. In the meantime I'm locking you in here."

"Do you have to?" Valerie asked.

"Yes," I said.

"Why can't we go with you?" Valerie pleaded.

She'd told me in Georgia that she had a fear of the dark. I'd already locked her in one closet, and she'd had a freaking panic attack.

Rosa realized whatever I was up to was not something she wanted any part of and took Valerie's arm and pulled her inside.

"Rosa," Valerie said, resisting.

I closed the closet door and locked it. It was Rosa's problem now. On my way out, I locked Rosa's office.

I took the backstairs because I didn't want the video camera to show that I'd left the suite. Valerie and Rosa would be my alibi that I had never left the floor.

Ray's office was on the floor below Rosa's. Unfortunately, I couldn't remember which side of the floor his office was on. I got lucky. The stairs let me out just a few feet from the empty hall and his open door

I opened the backpack, put on the gloves, gripped the knife, took a few steps, and walked into his office. He was surprised to see me.

"Kelly, what brings you down here?" he asked.

I took a quick look down the still vacant hall and then put my eyes back on him. He'd opened his drawer and had his hand half in. I'd gotten fucking lucky.

Still clutching the backpack, I released the knife and pulled out my gun. Thanks to Ray, I wouldn't have to use the dreaded knife. My plan had been to slit his throat. It wasn't a good plan because, one, it wouldn't be easy; two, I found the idea of slicing up a human being gross; three, I'd leave tons of evidence.

"Ray, bring out your gun slowly," I said. "I promise I won't hurt you."

I'm such a fucking liar. I closed the door behind me with my foot. He set a small gun on the desk in front of him.

"What's the second part, Ray?" I asked.

I picked up his gun. It already had a silencer on it. When things like this happen, I start believing in God.

"I have no idea what you're talking about," he said.

He obviously did because sweat ran down his face. In fact, I worried he might have a heart attack and die before I found out what I needed to know.

"Look," I said. "I think I've figured it out. I don't think you're behind it because you're not that kind of guy."

He shook his head. No, he wasn't like that at all.

"I didn't think so," I said. "Part one was Martinez. It was supposed to be Rosa, but I spooked Buddy when I showed up. So he framed Rosa."

Ray reluctantly nodded. He swallowed a couple times fast, and his Adam's apple twitched.

"Part two got triggered when Buddy died," I said. "Rosa gets killed because he wants to make sure she's out of Valerie's life."

"Did you kill Buddy?" he asked.

"You go first. Am I right?"

"It'll end right here. I tried to talk him out of it, but he was convinced she'd ruined Valerie. You and I can work out something."

"Start negotiating."

"I'll call off the hit. I'll give you two hundred fifty grand. No one will ever know anything."

"Hmm." I pretended to think about it. "The weak link in the whole thing is oddly enough the hit man. That's almost never the case. Because we're so fucking professional. Ray, I hate to tell you this, but we bought him and got Buddy's name."

Ray, realizing his fate, reddened. His upper lip trembled. Spit oozed out.

"That threw everything into chaos," I said. "He's gone rogue. I don't know if you can stop him. So, tell me, did I get part two right?"

"We figured Rosa would be in prison or out on bail when it happened. But it was part of the contract. It got triggered."

I shot Ray in the middle of the forehead. He fell sideways to the floor. I took off the silencer, went around the desk, brought his right hand up, and placed the gun in it. It was sloppy, but life isn't perfect.

TWENTY-SEVEN

I took off the gloves, threw them in the backpack, and trudged back into the hall and up the stairs, hoping I hadn't played too long with Ray.

Nothing looked out of the ordinary when I reached Rosa's office. Relieved, I unlocked the door, hurried to the closet, and flung it open. Rosa and Valerie tumbled out. Valerie was staggering and making weird human sounds. I grabbed her by her shirt collar and threw her against the wall. Her head hit the wall with a thud. My face was inches from hers. "Stop," I commanded through my teeth.

She crumpled to the floor, crying.

"Rosa, make her stop," I said.

Rosa gently shushed her. I pointed at Valerie and glared. "I'm calling down to the lobby," I said. "Quiet."

I picked up the phone. "Hey, Adam, this is Kell up in Rosa Gold's office. We're expecting a package. You see any delivery guys running around this morning?"

This shut up Valerie.

"Uh-huh," I said. "About what time? Do you know what company—?"

I briefly closed my eyes. "Okay. Thanks."

"Kell," Rosa said.

I put up my hand to silence her and faced the hallway. This

was fucking new for me. It's one thing to shoot someone in the head when they're unarmed, seated a few feet away from you. It's totally a different thing to shoot a moving target who's aiming at you. I sincerely regretted not practicing at the shooting range more often. I could have just lied to Gretchen. It's not like I hadn't already lied her to death.

"What's happening?" Valerie asked Rosa.

I waved her to be quiet, kept an eye on the hallway, and then motioned them down with my hand.

"Down on the floor," I said. "Behind the desk. Kneel, crouch down, and cover your head. Or get back in the closet."

"No fucking way," Valerie muttered.

They went to their knees behind the desk.

"Kell!" Before the flash and pain, I heard someone shout my name. I fell to my knees and instinctively raised my gun and fired.

The fucker was in the ceiling firing at me from above. It was a great idea, except he needed to kill me with the first or second bullet. He'd positioned himself flat on his stomach on the beams. Once he moved the ceiling panel and shot at me, he was a sitting duck. I mean, his fucking head was framed for me.

Rosa's yell saved me. It made me flinch, so he mostly missed me. I say mostly because his bullet creased the top of my skull, taking with it a small amount of hair and scalp and knocking me to my knees. I was saved again when I went down because his second shot flew over me and slammed into the wall. I took one clean shot and got him good between the eyes.

The room went quiet. Ken's dead eyes stared at me until I toppled to my side.

My head burned like a motherfucker. I repositioned myself to lie flat on the floor, eyes closed. Rosa roughly took hold of my arms and brought me up inches from her face. "Are you all right?" she asked, shooting hot breaths on my face with each word.

I opened my eyes.

"Kell?"

"She's bleeding," Valerie said.

Blood hit the floor in rhythmic, sickening taps. Thank God it wasn't mine. Ken's head was spilling blood like a spigot. It sickened me. I wrestled away from Rosa, rolled on my side, and covered my mouth, trying to talk myself out of throwing up.

"Please tell me you're all right," Rosa said.

I hate throwing up. I especially hate throwing up in front of people. Valerie has her fear of the dark. Rosa's got her hospitals. My worst fear is throwing up in public. It's got a name. Emetophobia.

"Call 911," Rosa said to Valerie. "Say we need an ambulance."

That got it out of my system. I'm not as bad as Rosa, but I don't like hospitals. "No." I gripped Rosa's arm hard. "Call Sylvia. Get her down here."

Rosa waited with me while Valerie volunteered to go down to the lobby to meet Sylvia. She couldn't wait to get away from the dead guy dripping blood from the ceiling.

"Why do you always have to get shot in the head?" Rosa asked, scrutinizing the wound.

"How bad is it?"

"It doesn't look deep. It's a little groove. Not as bad as the one Valerie gave you. He could have killed you." She shuddered. "This is awful, awful stuff."

"Before they come up here, I need to tell you some things. You decide how much to tell Valerie."

She nodded.

"Part two was that you'd be killed when Buddy died," I said.

Rosa took it stoically.

"They assumed you'd be out on bail or in prison when it happened, but—"

"He wanted to control it from beyond the grave," Rosa said, paling. No one wants to think that another person hates you enough to pay to have you killed. Even after they're dead.

"You got it from Ray?" she asked.

I nodded and gave her a meaningful look. "He committed suicide."

"There's a lot of that going around."

It made me laugh. It was the way she said it and the fact I hadn't had any sleep and had just been shot in the head. I pulled myself together because I didn't want Sylvia to think that I was the sort of person who thought the scene she was walking into was the least bit funny.

"Rosa, give me my wallet from the backpack and hide the backpack. Quick." It occurred to me that the cops might look through my stuff. You think they'd find it suspicious if they found gloves, a knife, and a silencer?

Rosa handed me my wallet, shoved the backpack in a desk drawer, and locked it. I motioned her to me.

"Look, Rosa, we need to get on the same page," I said. "I never left this floor since we got here. And a dude called you last night and said you were next. Got it?"

She nodded.

"I never spoke to him," I continued. "He threatened you and said you were next. Make sure Valerie understands."

Valerie arrived with Sylvia and a big guy who looked like a cop. I stiffened.

"This is my husband, Ron," Sylvia said. "I thought I should bring him when Valerie said there'd been a shooting."

Larry was right. Ron looked like him. He nodded at Rosa and me. We nodded back. He folded his arms and took that familiar cop stance.

"Do you need an ambulance?" Sylvia asked, noticing the damp blood on my scalp.

"No," I said.

My eyes went up to the ceiling. Their eyes followed mine. Sylvia didn't say anything, but breathed deeply. She looked at Ron and must have communicated telepathically because he stepped into the hall and made a phone call. I couldn't hear what he said.

"I have to tell you something," I said.

Sylvia intently looked at me.

"There's a possible suicide on the floor below," I said. Sylvia's face remained immobile. "The guy in the ceiling might have something to do with it. He's probably the same guy who called and threatened Rosa's life last night."

She blinked and waited for more. There wasn't any.

"Anything else you want to tell me?" she asked.

I shook my head. I liked that she could keep up and nothing made her hysterical.

"I thought you were bullshitting me when you said you were a bodyguard," she said. Sylvia looked up at the ceiling at the grotesque sight of Ken. "You are fucking good at this."

"I call her Wonder Girl," Rosa said.

I was queasy. My mouth was dry, and I felt like a boiled noodle.

"When the cops come," Sylvia said, "I'm the only one talking." She looked at Rosa and me. "Understand." We nodded. "Neither of you will say one damn word. Not even hello or goodbye. Now, listen to me carefully, Kell. Do you have a carry permit for the gun?"

"Yes."

"Great. There won't be any problem with the gun, right?"

"I'm licensed in Georgia and Illinois to carry a concealed weapon."

"Good. Florida recognizes Georgia's permits. Ever been convicted of anything?"

"Nothing."

"Ever been arrested?"

"Never. Could you get me something to drink, please, Rosa?"

I asked. My lips were sticking together. I licked them, but they felt like pieces of dry rubber.

"Sure," she said. "Sylvia, you want anything?"

"Diet Coke, please."

Rosa hustled out of the room and asked Ron if he wanted something. She was back moments later with Diet Cokes for Sylvia and Ron and a Dr. Pepper for me. I fumbled to open the can. My muscles were weak. I was shaking. Things were hitting me.

Rosa took the can from me and opened it. I drank quickly. Pop ran down my chin. Sylvia reached inside her blue leather purse and brought out a tissue. I finished the can and set it on the floor. Sylvia dabbed at my mouth, chin, and shirt with the tissue.

I burped but tried to conceal it. "Excuse me," I mumbled.

"Stay on the floor when the police come," Sylvia said. "Don't try to stand." Dressed in a smart navy blue skirt and blazer with matching heels, she carefully knelt down on the floor next to me. "I don't see you as the type who needs hand holding, but it'll look good for the cops." Sylvia smoothed her skirt and then slipped her hand into mine. I didn't mind. Considering what a force of nature she was, her hand felt tiny.

Ron stood in the hall facing the elevator. He occasionally glanced in at us. His arms were crossed again which made him seem even larger. He really did remind me of Larry. Even dressed like him. Dark windbreaker and blue jeans. Tan work boots. I couldn't wait to tell Larry that he was a type, but I figured he already knew.

Ron nodded at Sylvia. "They're here," Sylvia said, squeezing my hand. I thought it was cool how they communicated without talking. I'd love to see them argue.

"Remember to keep your fucking mouth shut, honey," Sylvia whispered.

TWENTY-EIGHT

Sylvia took charge. She was a dervish, all the while holding my hand. The cops apparently knew who she was, feared her, and treaded lightly. Even with a dead guy in the ceiling. Amazing.

It was nice sitting there, not having to talk. I could easily see myself blabbing things that didn't sound so good. I went Zen and removed myself while stuff went on around me until the cops insisted on calling paramedics to look at my head.

I convinced the dyke and straight guy who arrived that I was fine. "You were lucky," the dyke told me. I agreed. She wasn't my type, but we flirted a bit.

The cops kept my gun. I wasn't happy about it.

"Rosa, it makes me nervous not to have a gun," I whispered.

"I'll talk to Sylvia," she said.

Sylvia shook her head twice while Rosa talked to her. So much for that, I thought.

Rosa came back to me. "She put the kibosh on getting you another gun, but said she'll try to get yours back. For now, she'll make sure the house is guarded twenty-four-seven."

That made me feel better. Sylvia took such a liking to me that she took me back to her Collins Avenue condo after the police interviews. Ron went home with Rosa and Valerie until the security detail showed up.

The condo must have cost a few million. We were way, way

up, maybe on the thirtieth floor or higher. The view of Miami and the ocean was incredible.

After a shower, Sylvia let me wear one of Ron's white dress shirts while she washed my clothes. It was huge on me, more like a robe than a shirt.

I sat on her white couch, petting her white Maltese named Teddy. The little guy took an instant liking to me and literally jumped into my surprised arms. I looked at the ocean and thought about how much I missed that little bastard Thuggie.

"You and Rosa have a long distance relationship?" Sylvia asked.

"We're friends."

She didn't say anything.

"Rosa and Valerie are together," I clarified. "I live with Gretchen."

"I misunderstood. I'm sorry." She didn't sound like she bought it. "Valerie's the niece of Buddy Bach?"

"Yes."

I turned to see the expression on her face. She didn't have one. That was cool.

"Gretchen's got a Ph.D. in English. She's a college professor. We're on the outs now, but I think we'll get back together."

I don't know why I kept talking. Sylvia couldn't be that interested in my life.

"We've got a little dog named Thuggie," I said. "He's a Shih Tzu mix. A big fat cat too named Bella. They're in California right now with her."

"Rosa's lucky to have you. I have paperwork to fill out if you decide to work for me."

Sylvia reached into a white louvered credenza, pulled out papers, and handed them to me. I glanced down and saw Employment Application at the top. She must have seen the look of dismay on my face because she said, "You don't have to fill them out right now. Take everything with you."

I nodded and laid the papers on her glass end table next to a neat stack of coloring books.

"Those aren't mine," she said, pointing to them. "I have grandchildren. They come here every other weekend." She smiled. "They haven't realized yet that I'm to be feared. By the way, we have another interview tomorrow with the police."

"Can I go home after that?"

"I'll ask," she said. "You want to go back to Georgia?"

"Yes."

"Can I ask you a question, Kell? It's on the personal side."

"Go ahead." I figured I knew what she'd ask. I was wrong.

"What do you tell your mother you do?"

"My parents died when I was sixteen. It was a car accident."

"I'm sorry."

I shrugged. "If she were still here, I'd probably say I work in security. How many kids do you have?" I wanted to veer the conversation away from me. I don't like to talk about my parents. I can't find the right words to describe them. They come off sounding like hippies, and that's not a true picture of them.

"I had six children," she said.

Sylvia laughed at my expression and sat on the couch next to me. She reached over and stroked under Teddy's chin. His eyes squinted. "I got married young and had four kids in four years."

Gin told me to pay close attention to the intimate personal details someone tells you right off the bat because that'll tell you how they think of themselves, what they think are the most important details about their own story. It's called self-disclosure.

"My husband left me for his secretary, so I moved from New Jersey to Miami—I'd put him through Seton Hall while we were married—and got my degree here. I married my law partner right out of school and had two more children."

"You had lots of energy," I said.

She shrugged. "It didn't seem so at the time, but I must have, huh? Anyway, he went gay, and we divorced. We still adore each other, which is good."

She hesitated because she wanted to tell me something painful. I figured it had to do with the "I had six children" statement. I looked at her and waited.

"I have five children now, six grandchildren. I had a daughter who got involved in drugs in high school here in Miami. My youngest. She died when she was eighteen. She was a sensitive person and had a hard time, I guess, with life."

"I'm sorry," I said.

We stayed quiet for a long time. Silence rarely bothers me. It bothers most people though. I was curious how long it'd take Sylvia to say something. It took her a lot longer than most people.

"You were young when your parents died," she said. "Do you have siblings?"

"I have a sister. She's married to Larry. It's a complicated thing. I wasn't raised with her, and we didn't connect till a few years ago. We didn't know about each other until then."

"That sounds like a TV movie."

"It played out like that too. Anyway, she's got a Ph.D. in psychology and teaches college in California. We're different, but we're trying. Rosa's more like my family than anyone else. I've known her longest."

"I'm a big fan of Larry's."

"Me too. I wasn't sure about him at first, but he's cool. Don't tell him I said that."

I'd told Sylvia more than I'd probably told anyone in such a brief amount of time. I'm not a big self-disclosure freak. I suspected Sylvia wasn't either.

After that, we got down to business. Sylvia prepped me on what to expect the next day. She was softer with me than she'd been the first day that Rosa and I met her. Still, she made it clear it was her way or the highway. I was fine with it. She obviously knew tons more than I did about the legal system. I've never had a problem following the advice of experts. I can be cocky about my own area of expertise, but I know when I'm out of my league.

Sylvia wanted me to see her condo to let me know that she was tremendously successful, that she knew exactly what she was doing. I was convinced.

TWENTY-NINE

"We're all okay, Larry. The hit man is dead. So is Ray, Uncle Buddy, and Aunt Marie." I couldn't remember what he knew. I was exhausted.

Sylvia had just dropped me off at Rosa's in her white BMW. I called Larry before I crashed.

"Anyone else?" he finally asked.

"No. Like I said, we're okay. I got shot in the head, but it's minor. Didn't even need to go to the hospital."

"He got a shot off," he said with regret.

"Two."

"I shouldn't have left."

"No. This isn't your thing. I'm sorry I brought you into it. I needed you though. Things wouldn't have turned out the same if you hadn't been here. That's for sure. You probably saved my life. And Rosa's. Maybe Valerie's. I still haven't figured everything out. Anyway, I just want to go home. By the way, thanks for hooking us up with Sylvia. She's worth her weight in gold." I remembered how small she was. "Twice her weight. She took me up to her condo afterwards. Did you know she's a grandmother?"

"I figured."

"She told me her daughter died when she was eighteen."

"Suicide."

"I guessed drug overdose by the way she described it."

"I'm sure it was suicide," Larry said. "From what I understand, Sylvia found her. I also heard that her daughter was gay. You haven't been charged with anything, have you?"

"No. Everything's fine. Anyway, I didn't get much sleep last night. I'll tell you the details later."

"I definitely want to hear them. By the way, what happened between you and Gretchen yesterday?"

Was it yesterday? "Why?"

"She's on the warpath again. What'd you do?"

"I kind of hung up on her."

"She's kind of enraged again. Better come up with something good."

"Any ideas?" I couldn't think straight.

"Tell her your car broke down," he said.

That'll work?"

"What else you got?"

"I'm tired, Larry. I just want her to put up with me. Is that asking too much?"

He didn't say anything.

"Anyway," I said, "I wanted to call and let you know. We'll talk later."

We hung up, and I immediately called Gretchen.

"Yes," she answered, with that clipped tone I was getting used to.

"I'm sorry, Gretchen," I blurted. "When we were talking yesterday, I was in the car, and it just died on me. Right on 78. I had to call a tow truck and—"

"Are you okay?" Bless her heart, she bought it.

"Yeah. I got it towed to T & G. It turned out to be some weird electrical thing."

"Is it fixed or could it happen again?"

"No," I said, surprising myself. "It's fixed. It was like a—I don't know how to explain it." I really didn't. "I'm sorry I hung up so abruptly. I just freaked out when it died on me. I mean, I was right in the middle of 78."

"Okay. Thanks for explaining. I wondered what happened to you. Hey, I'm kind of in the middle of something. Can I call you back?"

"Yeah, but—"

"What?"

"I haven't been sleeping. I'm taking a nap and turning off the phone. Don't freak out if you call, and I don't answer."

"Are you sleeping at all, babe?"

"Yeah. Just, you know, off and on. But I've hit a wall and need to lie down."

"You think you're coming down with something?" she asked. I never napped unless I was sick.

"No. Just tired. Not enough sleep."

"All right. Get some sleep."

I slept for a few hours and then slid out of bed and ambled into the kitchen. Rosa and Valerie were drinking coffee. While Valerie poured me a cup, I pulled out the employment application from my backpack.

"What's that?" Rosa asked.

I stared at the application. "I have to fill this out for Sylvia. It's an employment app."

"Want me to do it?" Rosa asked.

Hell, yes. I pushed the paper toward her. I hate doing stuff like this. Back in the day, Rosa took care of most of my paperwork, except for paying bills. Even now, I still send her my tax stuff.

Rosa started filling out the application immediately. She actually enjoys this stuff.

"What's Gretchen's last name?" she asked.

"Wolf. W-O-L-F."

"What's her cell phone?"

"What are you filling out?"

"Who to contact in case of an emergency."

"Don't you think it should be you?"

"There's a space for two. I put me first."

"Okay." I gave her Gretchen's cell phone number.

Rosa hesitated, tapping the pen on her cheek. "Maybe I should have put your sister."

I shook my head. "No."

"Larry?"

I thought about it. "You'd know to contact Larry, right?"

"Of course, sweetie. I'm putting down that you have a masters in psychology."

"I never actually finished it."

"Close enough."

"It's in your name, not mine."

"She won't ask for transcripts, Kell. It's fine. You were the one who did the work."

"No. Put that that I have a B.A. in psychology. Don't give me the masters. It's a lie."

"Sweetie, everyone lies on these things."

"Really?" I asked.

She nodded. I looked at Valerie.

"It's true, Kell," Valerie said.

Rosa was almost giddy. "Jacob claims a Ph.D. in art history on his resume." Jacob, Rosa's older brother, owned a historical restoration company in New York.

"It's not like anyone will ever check it out," Valerie said.

"If she did, I'd look bad," I said.

Rosa was impatient with me. "Since you want me to fill it out, I'm doing it the way I want."

Fine. It was better that she fill it out. "I'll tell the truth if she asks me," I said.

"Go ahead," Rosa said. "Blame me if you want."

I waited for Valerie to leave the room before I told Rosa about the conversation I'd shared with Sylvia at her condo. "She thought we were together," I said.

"I'm not surprised," Rosa said. "A lot of people think that. You know, the way we interact. We act like we're lovers."

"Hmm."

That night the three of us curled up like puppies on the bed. Rosa and Valerie had taken Ambien. This was huge for Rosa because she's militantly anti-prescription. Rosa offered me one, but I turned it down. I'm even more anti-prescription than Rosa.

They quickly fell asleep, but I kept going over the day's events in my head. I was stupid to turn down the pill and thought about going through Rosa's medicine cabinet to find one when I finally drifted off, only to wake again at three.

I kept going over all the mistakes I'd made. There'd been plenty. We were lucky we hadn't been killed. It would have been my fault too.

The biggest mistake I made was when I put Rosa and Valerie on the office floor, leaving them defenseless. Still, it would have been stupid to move them out of the office or to another room because I had no idea where he was.

After going over it again, I decided the best thing would have been to shove them back in the office closet. They would have been safest there. Of course, if I'd done this, Rosa wouldn't have alerted me, and Ken would have killed me and then gone after Rosa. These kinds of thoughts made it impossible for me to go back to sleep.

I carefully extricated myself from Rosa and Valerie. They barely stirred. I put on Rosa's robe in case one of the security dudes was looking in the windows and went to the kitchen laptop where I pulled up *The Miami Herald*.

We were front page news. The details were sketchy. They hadn't identified Ken yet, and there was no connection to Uncle

Buddy and Aunt Marie. In fact, if you read the newspaper report without knowing what was going on you'd have a hard time understanding what happened. I was remarkably uninterested. I mainly checked to make sure my name wasn't in it. It wasn't. Sylvia was great.

I went to my email and was surprised to see a message from Gretchen. It'd come in an hour earlier which would have been eleven California time. It had no subject heading. I opened it, hoping she wasn't dumping me in an email. I'd never get back to sleep.

"Whenever I talk to you on the phone, I don't say half of what I planned to say," she wrote. "There's something about your voice that makes me pull back. Today, especially, you seemed distant, almost numb. I guess, like me, you're protecting yourself. It keeps me off-balance. It makes me not want to be vulnerable with you. See, here again, it seems we're having difficulty communicating. Couples therapy might help us do better. Anyway, I do want you to know that I miss you. A lot. More than I thought I would. I was angry when I left, but I find now that I'm just hurt. Kell, I'm leaving tomorrow and driving back. Nothing's decided, but we need to talk face to face."

If Gretchen was headed back, I needed to get my butt out of Miami. I'd ask Sylvia to convince the authorities to let me go home.

I returned to bed. Rosa and Valerie were still asleep. I climbed in next to Rosa and pressed against her. She adjusted and murmured.

THIRTY

I was officially given the all-clear from the police. They reached some weird conclusions. I didn't give a fuck. All I knew was that I wasn't a suspect and could go home.

Believe it or not, they decided the Bach murder-suicide was coincidental to everything else. To them, it was a clear case of an elderly couple checking out because of a multitude of health issues. Ironically, Uncle Buddy made a mistake getting hospitalized the day Herb Martinez got killed. The cops figured the "heart attack" was the final straw for a man with failing health and an ailing wife.

As for Ray, they figured the suicide was faked. I didn't do my best work there, but they concluded it was set up by Ken. They also gave Ken credit for Martinez's murder which was the only one he deserved. The Miami police department wanted to wrap up everything like a burrito. I suspect Sylvia pressured them to clear Rosa.

I learned more about Ken. In some ways, he was like me. His real name was Kenyon Dill. He had a college degree, an expensive house in the suburbs, and the neighbors never suspected he was a bad guy. He lived with a dude who claimed he had no idea Ken was a hit man. Ken had no arrest record and listed his occupation as a security consultant. Just like me.

I talked to Larry about it before I left Miami. "He got bored," he said on the phone. "Wanted to spice things up. That's why he fucked with you."

"He was greedy," I said. "Think about it, Larry. He put himself in a position to get three fees. He couldn't turn down the money."

"Boredom plus greed equals death—let that be a lesson to you, Kell."

Boredom plus greed divided by stupidity. "Valerie and Rosa are at the funeral," I said, wanting to change the topic.

"Awkward doesn't even begin to describe that scenario," Larry said.

"Rosa said she wasn't going, but Valerie told her it'd look better if she did. Rosa said 'Fuck that. I'm phony, but I'm not that phony.' Anyway, she ended up going, mainly to avoid raising suspicion among family members."

"It's time for you to get out of there, Kell."

"I know."

"Hope Gretchen doesn't find out anything."

"Me too."

I couldn't look Sylvia in the eye when I handed her my application. She raised an eyebrow a few times while she skimmed it, but didn't question me on anything.

Sylvia's offer was generous. I figured it might be an appropriate transition from what I was doing with Larry.

Rosa approved. "I see it as a good thing for you," she said.

"I don't know what else to do," I said.

"You can do it.," Rosa said. "You did the school thing. You were fine."

"It was a game, Rosa. I played the game."

"Everything is a game, Kell. Find something that keeps you out of trouble. You've been lucky so far." Rosa gave me a look.

The three of us had sex my last night in Miami. Rosa and Valerie seemed to be going through the motions, and maybe I was too.

I left early the next morning and arrived in Stone Mountain at four p.m. Nicole Westlake's truck was in the driveway. Like I said before, she's my gardener and looks out for the property when I'm away.

"Hey, Nicole," I said, when I caught up with her in the back yard. "Listen, I hate to put you in this position, but my being out town for a while, well, I don't want Gretchen to know."

She gave me a look. That's one of the things I like about Nicole. You always know where you stand with her. She couldn't hide her feelings if she tried, and she didn't try.

"Let's hope it doesn't come up," she said.

Okay, she wouldn't lie for me. That was cool. I understand her point.

Anyway, I doubted the subject would come up because Gretchen doesn't like Nicole. She never got over her suspicion that something had gone on with Nicole and me before she came into the picture. Nothing had because Nicole told me the first day we met she was with someone, and that was that.

"I know you won't out and out lie," I said, "but, really, if we could keep it quiet. She thinks I've been here the whole time. I'm afraid it'll blow up things if she finds out I wasn't."

I wanted to tell her that I hadn't done anything bad when I was gone, but it was a lie, and I didn't want to lie to her. Still, I don't like disappointing her.

"I have my head back on straight," I said. "I want another chance with her."

Nicole liked that. "We've all made mistakes."

I almost started hyperventilating when Gretchen's car pulled up in the driveway. It had been a long time since we'd seen each other, and I didn't know what to expect.

Thuggie ran in like a madman when I opened the door and kept jumping up and bouncing off me. You'd think I'd paid him, he was so fucking thrilled to see me. Gretchen, not so much. She hugged me, but that was it. In fact, she got irritated with Thuggie.

"That's enough, Thuggie," she said twice.

Then he went on a barking rampage directed at me. Like he blamed me for two long car trips locked up with Bella.

Gretchen checked out the kitchen like a fucking detective. "It doesn't look like you ate anything but cereal," she said.

"I've been eating out."

"You haven't been eating right, have you?"

I didn't say anything.

Gretchen put her stuff in the bedroom and told Thuggie to shut his little fucking mouth. Then we sat on the bed because she said we needed to talk right then.

"Did you sleep with anyone while I was gone?" she asked.

"No." Okay, it's a technicality. Rosa and Valerie are two. Not one. She asked about any*one*. She'd flip her lid if I said yes, so I lied. But it wasn't a bald-faced lie. Yikes, we didn't start off well, did we?

"I did, Kell."

I knew there was a possibility, but figured Gretchen would be too something to do it.

"It was a mistake," she said. "I realized it and felt horrible. I wasn't over you. It was a disaster."

"Who was it?"

"An ex."

"Michelle?"

"Yes." Gretchen blushed. "I was stupid. I don't know what I was thinking. Did you get in contact with that Debra woman again?"

"No. I've told you. She's not in my life." I changed the subject. "What did Gin think about you sleeping with Michelle?" I asked.

"She thought it was a mistake. She's never liked Michelle."

"I'm sure she's down on me too, huh?" I hadn't talked to Gin since I left for Miami.

"She wants us to work things out."

"That's surprising."

"She doesn't approve of what you did, but she told me everyone deserves another chance. She thinks counseling is a great idea."

She was back on the fucking counseling.

"Uh-huh."

"Do you have a preference on the day or time we go?" Gretchen asked.

Fucking fuckster. "No."

"Gin thinks you've got stuff to work through. That maybe counseling will be the key."

"Uh-huh. Did you tell your parents and sister?"

"No. I didn't even let them know I was in town."

This was a fucking relief. I like her family and don't want them to think I'm a creep.

"You didn't call them?" I asked.

She shook her head. "I didn't want them to know I'd failed in the relationship."

"You didn't fail."

I kissed her. She let me. We ended up having some fucking epic sex. Rosa and Valerie hadn't ruined me, if you know what I mean. I'd been worried about that.

"What happened to your head?" Gretchen later asked in bed. I'm taller than her so she hadn't noticed the wound until now. She gently touched it. "It looks like you scratched it on something."

"I went up in the attic and caught it on the ceiling," I said.

She winced. "Ouch."

I nodded.

"What were you doing in the attic?" she asked.

"I was getting light bulbs." I have no idea where the lie came from.

"Oh." A puzzled look spread across her face. "I thought the light bulbs were in the pantry."

I looked at her. Should I bowl one more lie? I closed my eyes. I didn't have the energy for it.

"Kell?" she asked. "What's wrong?"

Should I just get it over with?

"I got shot in the head."

THIRTY-ONE

I opened my eyes. Gretchen pulled away from me and sat on the edge of the bed. The look on her face was priceless.

"You're joking, right?" she asked.

"I was in Miami. Someone tried to kill Rosa. I acted as her bodyguard."

"When I was in California?"

"Yes."

She got off the bed and took a couple steps backward. "You were in Miami when we were talking on the phone?"

"Yes."

"Why didn't you tell me?"

"I figured you'd flip out."

"When you said you had to get off the phone, you were doing your bodyguard stuff?"

"Yes."

"You were shot?"

"Yes."

"You realize this is an incredible story?"

"I'm sure it is," I said.

"What happened to the guy who shot you?"

We stared at each other for a long time.

"Kell?"

"I killed him."

"With a gun?"

"Yes. I shot him."

"Who was he?"

"A hit man."

"A hit man was trying to kill Rosa?" Gretchen seemed embarrassed to ask such a ridiculous thing.

"Yes. She'd already been framed for a murder she didn't commit."

Gretchen shook her head, like she was clearing her thoughts. "When did all this happen?"

"After you left. She called and asked me to come down because she was having problems." I needed to keep things vague. "Stuff escalated."

"Stuff escalated," Gretchen repeated in a weird voice. "Why'd she ask you?"

"I'd worked as a bodyguard for her company in Chicago." Gretchen knew this. I'd told her when we first got together that I had previously worked for Rosa.

"The first time I called you—"

"I was already in Miami," I said.

"But you acted like you were here. One time you said you were at the p-a-r-k."

"I lied. I didn't want to tell you because you'd worry."

Gretchen's face scrunched up, trying to make sense of what I was saying. "At what point did you get shot in the head?"

"The day after I abruptly got off the phone with you. I got off the phone because something happened. Rosa was in danger."

"So you got off the phone, got shot in the head, and killed a man."

I shouldn't have told her. Gretchen was horrified.

"Then you called me back and said you had to hang up with me because your car broke down. On 78. Had to take it to T & G. An electrical problem. Wow. I don't believe anyone else in the world is having this conversation right now."

"I couldn't tell you the truth, Gretchen."

"You can never tell me the truth. I don't know if I believe you now."

"Want proof?"

"How can you give me proof?"

I climbed out of bed. She started dressing. I did the same.

"I'll show you the news reports," I said.

Gretchen breathed uneasily. "God, I should have stayed in California. Why do I keep trying with you? Honest to God, Kell."

I picked up the iPad on the bedroom desk and brought up *The Miami Herald.* I tapped a few times to get the story, motioned her to sit in the chair, and handed her the iPad. She read. I carefully watched her body language as she scrolled down the page. With each news nugget, she stiffened.

"The newspaper didn't identify you by name," she said, keeping her back to me.

"You know it's me."

"They said you might be a target."

"The lawyer said that, so they wouldn't identify me. She's put me on retainer. She wants me under the radar."

"What about those other people who died?" Gretchen turned and looked at me.

"Gretchen, it was a dirty, nasty business. I don't understand everything that went down. I just know that someone framed Rosa and tried to kill her. She's my friend. I couldn't let anything happen to her."

"You stayed with her."

I knew where this was going. "With her and her girlfriend. They've been together a long time. Huge house. Lots of bedrooms."

"What did she do for you? I mean, you saved her life, took a bullet. What'd she do for you?"

"She paid me. It's business. She hired me."

"What'd she pay you?"

"$100,000."

This wasn't true. She'd paid me $250,000. The whole thing turned out to be expensive for Rosa. Sylvia's fee was a small fortune, as was Larry's. However, in typical Rosa fashion she came out ahead. Buddy's business transferred to Valerie upon his death. The big prize, though, is his estate which Valerie will inherit. It's worth millions of dollars. Rosa's net profit is huge.

"How many days were you there?" Gretchen asked.

I shook my head. "I've lost track. There were nights I didn't sleep. I could figure it out if it's important."

"What do you mean, the lawyer put you on retainer?" she asked.

"She wants me to occasionally work as a bodyguard for her clients. At least that's what I figure she wants."

"Is she gay?"

"No. She's about sixty. Married to a guy who looks like Larry. He's twenty years younger than her. She is not gay." I gave Gretchen a look. "You think everyone's gay."

"What she wants you to do is dangerous, isn't it?"

"She said it's more like babysitting. The only problem is I have to fly there when she calls."

"Were you planning to tell me?"

"Which part?"

She didn't like that.

I took a deep breath. "Gretchen, I've been doing jobs for a while. I don't mean with Larry. I mean outside the consulting thing I do with Larry. The thing in Atlanta—"

"When you cheated on me."

"I was on a job. I didn't meet her at the park."

"What kind of job?"

"A lot of the work I do is confidential. That means I sign a confidentiality agreement. I can't give you details."

Gretchen was principled. She'd accept this. "What job

requires you to sleep with someone?"

"It didn't. I did it because I thought the thing might fall apart if I didn't. I didn't do it because I couldn't control myself."

Gretchen shook her head. "Why did you call her the night I confronted you?"

"I didn't. I never saw or heard from her again after I left. I called Larry."

"*Larry*? Why would you call Larry?"

"For advice," I said.

"Why would you call Larry for advice?"

"He's a smart guy for one thing. And you and Gin are kind of the same."

"Your mind works in strange ways, Kell. What did he tell you?"

"Tell the truth."

"Why didn't you? Who are you really, honey?"

She didn't deliver the line with the same inflection, but it was the same exact words that Debra had used. How fucking ironic is that?

"I didn't think you'd stay if you found out," I said. "My worst fear was that you'd leave me. Want to know who I am? I'm someone who needs a certain amount of excitement and danger in my line of work, but I also need you. When I was at Rosa's, all I did was talk about you and how much I wanted to make it work." It wasn't *all* I did, but close enough to almost be true.

"What did she say?"

"She said, 'Tell the truth, Kell.'"

"God, I wished you'd stayed in academia."

"I wouldn't have been happy. I could have done it a while, but I know myself. I would have gone off track."

"Does the lawyer know about me?"

"Yes," I said. "I had to fill out paperwork for her. There was a section for who to contact. I put you down as my partner."

"How many times have you cheated on me because you were

on a job?"

"One time," I said, holding up my index finger. "God, Gretchen, it was a nightmare answering your questions. Honest to God, I was flailing, floundering. Everything I said made it worse."

She chuckled, glanced back at the iPad, and shook her head. "Someone should write a book about you." She motioned to me. "Let me see the wound."

I knelt at her feet. Her hand lightly caressed the top of my head near where the groove was. It didn't hurt anymore. It felt weird, like after a nerve has been damaged. Gretchen's hand reached across to the side of my head and felt a different scar. This one, from Valerie, was deeper. It'd healed up remarkably well, and I doubt anyone would have guessed it was a bullet wound. It was barely visible unless you, like Gretchen, knew where to look. I waited for the inevitable question.

"Why is it at a weird angle?" she asked, touching the more recent wound again.

"He was above me," I said, relieved, though I knew the unasked question was a ghost that could and probably would reappear.

"You mean you were kneeling." The image chilled her.

"He was in the ceiling."

Gretchen stroked my hair. "Were you scared?"

"Terrified."

"Somehow that's reassuring. You know I'll talk to Gin about this."

"I figured."

"Can you promise me two things if I stay?" Gretchen asked.

"I'm not sure." I figured I knew what they were, but I was wrong.

"First, you need to promise that whatever you do, you won't get hurt. Second, you won't get arrested."

"Obviously I don't want either to happen, but I'm not sure I can promise."

"You were lucky you weren't killed. I have a feeling you were lucky you weren't arrested too." Gretchen continued to play with my hair. "Will this Sylvia woman ask you to do anything illegal or dangerous?"

"She's a lawyer. A well-known lawyer. She's married to a guy who used to be a U.S. Marshal."

"That's not convincing me."

"She has way too much to lose. Also, she likes me." I lifted my head up and smiled. "She's like a mother figure to me."

THIRTY-TWO

"Well, Kell got shot in the head."

True to her word, Gretchen called Gin, and this is how I imagined she started the conversation. After an hour, she joined me, Thuggie, and Bella in the living room with the results.

"Gin thinks you have a thrill-seeking disorder," Gretchen said. "Well, not a disorder so much as a compulsion to do dangerous, risky things. Even the time you spent in California in the graduate program pretending to be someone you weren't is a symptom of it. She said people like you have an area of the brain called the insula that gets activated."

"Is it curable?"

"She doesn't think so. She thinks it stems from your childhood and unresolved grief. She thinks you should be in counseling." God, it was always counseling with these two.

Gretchen smiled and made a face. "She said exactly what I thought she'd say. Do you remember what I told you when you said it'd be okay if I quit teaching? I said I'd get fat and end up crazy. If I tell you that you can't do what you want to do, the same thing will happen to you. I don't think you'll get fat, but you'll get bored and depressed. Even stupid Freud said everyone needs love and work to be happy."

Gretchen had been back for only a few days, but we quickly

returned to our familiar routine. I was thrilled.

I was at the park with Thuggie when my phone rang. It was Gin.

"Kell, Gretchen told me you got—you were injured." Gin couldn't even say the word 'shot.'

Thuggie pulled hard, trying to catch a pack of four standard poodles walking ahead of us. He hates them. I don't particularly like them either, but I can control myself. He can't. I picked up his barking puppy ass and walked the other way.

"I'm okay," I said. It wasn't easy carrying him and talking to Gin.

"I'm glad. I can't believe you got—she said it didn't look bad."

I didn't say anything.

"You're not talking much," she said.

"Sorry." I put Thuggie back on the ground and gave him a look.

"Are you angry with me?"

"Why would I be angry?"

"Kell, I hope you and Gretchen make it work. I really do. I was angry when I found out you cheated on her."

"Okay."

"You think I should have stayed out of it."

"You did what you thought you should do."

"It might have seemed like I abandoned you. That wasn't my intention. I don't want you to ever feel that way. I'm sorry."

"What?" Yeah, I wanted hear it again.

"I apologize for the way I handled things."

That was big of her. "I accept your apology."

"It was Larry who made me realize I screwed up."

Good old Larry. "In fact, he made me see how it looked to you. It was enlightening."

I grinned. "Imagine that."

"Sometimes I get protective of Gretchen, maybe

overprotective. I should have been more supportive of you. It's a hard balance for me. My sister and my best friend. Anyway, I wanted to communicate to you—" Her voice broke. Oh, boy.

"It's okay."

She took a deep breath. "Gretchen tells me you'll be working for a Miami lawyer. I Googled her. She sounds interesting. I wouldn't mind doing some expert witness work. Put in a good word for me."

"I will."

"How dangerous will it be, Kell?"

"Not very."

"I don't want you getting killed."

"Me either."

"When do you start working for her?"

"I'm not sure. I'm on retainer, so I have to be ready to go."

"I have some time off. Would you mind if I came and visited? I know you and Gretchen need to work on things, but I was thinking in a month or so. We haven't seen each other since you and Gretchen came out here for the wedding. Larry could probably get away too. You haven't seen him in a while either."

That was fucking funny.

"It's a great idea," I said.

It was a red letter day in the Kell Digby household because only a few minutes later I got a call from Rosa.

"Guess who asked about you today?" she asked. "Risa Rispoli. Unfortunately, when I told her you got back with your girlfriend, she got all tudey on me and said, 'Figures.'"

"And how are things with you?" I asked.

"Okay. Valerie's taking over the real estate company after we get back from Greece. She needs a project."

"What do you plan to do?"

Rosa didn't answer right away. "Don't freak out. We're thinking about moving to Atlanta."

I stopped walking Thuggie.

"You're freaking out, aren't you? I promise I won't mess up anything you have with Gretchen."

"Why would you do that?" I asked, continuing our walk after getting a dirty look from Thuggie. He wanted to catch up to the poodles.

If Gretchen met Rosa and Valerie, she'd have more questions than a fucking kid at a fucking zoo. Did I really think Gretchen wouldn't pick up on something?

"What about the company?" I asked.

"Once Valerie gets everything under control, it seems we could live anywhere."

"Why Atlanta?"

Rosa chuckled. "You sound suspicious."

"No. Curious."

"I was under the radar for years, Kell. I go legit, and everything goes flooey. I feel like I'm being watched here."

"You're fucking with me, right?"

"It would bother you that much?"

"Why Atlanta?"

"It's a great place, sweetie. Full of opportunities."

I laughed. I acted amused, but, yes, I was freaked out. Hopefully it'd turn out to be one of those things Rosa talked about but never did.

"If we relocate there," Rosa said, "I want you to think about working for us. I think you'd like it."

Why does everyone think I want a career in real estate? I don't care a thing about it.

"Oh, and Dana would come with us. We've hired her full-time."

Great.

"You're afraid to have Gretchen meet me, aren't you?" she asked.

"Yes."

"Is she as open as you?"

I knew what she meant. "No."

"You never know."

"I know. Are you still in touch with Larry?" I asked, changing the subject.

"Of course. He's a great guy. His detective agency idea sounds interesting. Maybe we could do a combination real estate-detective agency. Like that place you told me about."

Not far from where I live, there's a combination hair salon and do-it-yourself pesticide place. I'm not lying. It's run by a husband-and-wife team.

"Is Valerie okay?" I asked.

Rosa sighed. "She's going with the euthanasia angle."

"I can see that."

"It's tragic."

I couldn't tell if Rosa was being ironic. "She'll be all right," she said. "She's a tough girl."

"I can't screw this thing up with Gretchen, Rosa. I was miserable without her."

Rosa remained quiet. She probably wanted to remind me that I didn't act all that miserable, but Rosa knew when it was best to keep her mouth shut. She could say a lot without saying anything.

"I'm better when I'm with her," I said.

"Then don't screw it up."

"I need to stop doing bad girl stuff."

"I understand."

I wondered if she did. "I can't do anything that would entail lying to her," I said.

"Got it, Kell. She's good for you. She'll never understand you, but you need someone to keep you grounded."

"If you were to move here, when would it be?"

"It's just a possibility. Don't worry. I promise I won't mess up what you have with Gretchen."

This was the second time she'd said that. Sometimes the way Rosa says something makes me nervous, and this was one of those times. She had something in her head that she wasn't sharing with me.

"I want you to be happy, sweetie" she said. "That's what I've always wanted."

"Uh-huh."

Rosa giggled.

Even Rosa's threat to move to Atlanta couldn't ruin my spirits. Things were back to normal, at least as close to normal as they'd probably get.

The big trouble spot that loomed ahead was the counseling session. Gretchen had scheduled it for the following week. My hope was that Sylvia would call and give me a reason to get my ass out of Georgia.

I mean, seriously, can you see me in counseling?

THE END

I hope you've enjoyed reading *Killing Rosa*. It is the sequel to *Black-Hearted Bitch*, the first title in the Kell Digby Crime Novel series.

Black-Hearted Bitch is hard-boiled noir. Hit man Kell Digby has been killing for so long she's become bored. Sent from Chicago to Atlanta for a routine hit, the assignment goes bad. Brutally betrayed, she's content to nurse her wounds until she's lured back to life with an irresistible con game involving a sister she never knew she had. A runner-up in the 2013 Rainbow Awards, critics have called this novel "suspenseful," "entertaining," "tight, well written," and "edgy."

Relative Innocence is a dark, suspenseful mystery about a spree killer's son, a suspected serial killer's daughter, and the attorney who befriends them. It's been described as having "a great plot, believable characters and plenty of twists and turns to keep you guessing till the last page. You won't want it to end."

In *Tighter, Tighter*, future rock star Kath Branch, then a teenager, disappears from St. James, Illinois in 1975. That same night, local sandwich shop owner Billy Carlson is gunned down and dumped in the St. James River. The cold case is personal for prosecutor Meredith Carlson because Billy was her husband's father. Convinced she's solved the case, Meredith lures Kath back to her hometown for the first time since she left thirty-five years ago. Meredith has no idea she's about to unearth shocking secrets about herself and her family. *Tighter, Tighter* received an Honorable Mention in the 2012 Rainbow Awards. "... brilliantly plotted, with startling twists. Loved this book, totally sucks you in."

All my books are available at Amazon and wherever books are sold. Please visit my website, lynnkear.com, and follow me on Facebook and Twitter.

www.ingramcontent.com/pod-product-compliance
Lightning Source LLC
Chambersburg PA
CBHW021031130626
46552CB00005B/1783